A Long Road to Nowhere

Les Drew

About the Author:

Leslie Allen Drew was born in a small sea-side town in West Sussex back in the 50s. With countryside all around and the South Downs just a bicycle ride away he would spend hours on-end out across the Brooks and Water Meadows around the River Arun. Camping with friends, cooking wild duck eggs, frying-up sausages and generally running around like a bunch of wild 'injuns.

In his twenties he began work building greenhouses, not the little garden-type ones but huge, big horticultural things covering acres & acres of land. These were all across the south-coast; New Milton in the New Forest, Wimborne in Dorset, Cullompton in Devon, Chew Magna near Bath and many others – hence his affinity with the West Country.

He did a variety of other work after getting married; a chef, a milkman, a kitchen equipment salesman, Pickfords Removals, parcels deliveries and anything else that could make money. He qualified as an Accountant some years ago and ran a successful accountancy practice locally.

Throughout all this time he was a paid-up member of The Goon Show Preservation Society and through this he met his comedy hero Spike Milligan several times, along with Harry Secombe and Michael Bentine. He helped with research on TV shows about the Goons and was often called on by BBC Radio Sussex to comment on the stars of the Goon Show.

This came to its peak with an Invitation to (the then) Prince Charles' 70th Birthday Party at Buckingham Palace "By Royal Appointment", which the Radio station wanted a report on the radio, live, the very next day… which was fun.

He is married and has two children and four grandchildren and has now retired.

Cover art by Paul Murphy Design Ltd.

Publishing help by:
Lee Cooke Computing and Design
Worthing
West Sussex
www.leecooke.co.uk / hq@leecooke.co.uk

This is the author's first fiction book.

A catalogue record for this book is available from the British Library.

A Long Road to Nowhere / L A Drew. -- 1st Edition
Published 2025

ISBN 978-1-0684645-0-8

Dedicated to my wife Kay,

my daughters Louise and Helen,

and grandchildren

Bailey, Alana, Corben and Jensen

Chapter 1

George, Mollie & Missy

Isn't it funny how things just seem to fall into place. You don't give it much thought, then suddenly it seems the right thing to do, the right time to do it. No reason, no explanation, it just feels right. It's a bit like the first appearance of the new shoots after Winter; the daffodils, snowdrops and crocus tips popping up out of the frosty ground from their cold dark hiding places. New buds appearing on the trees. Cuckoos in the woods calling out for a mate, the dawn chorus getting louder and more purposeful every day. Some say it's just the warmer weather switching everything on, the on-set of Spring with its lighter evenings bringing a new joy to the day. Mother Nature herself waking up from her long slumber, the cycle of the planets in their ellipses around the sun, the circle of Life, that sort of thing.

Of course it was all of these, and more. His own feelings of the change from Winter to Spring were always undecided. Like everyone, Sam knew it would happen, although he didn't know when it would happen, not precisely, him not being a man of the times with diaries and calendars and things to remind him, so he just waited until it did.

And today it felt like Spring had happened.

He woke up as usual at 5 o'clock although at this time of the year it was still dark. Quietly making his way down to the kitchen for his early morning cup of tea he was surprised to see the little three-wheeled electric milk-float silently trundling up the driveway, its lights all twinkling in the early morning gloom.

"Better put three tea bags in" he mumbled softly to himself as he watched the cheerful walk of the milkman, gamely heaving a full crate of milk up the gravel path to the back door. He was a young lad, only about twenty-three, not many peoples' idea of a milkman, he still had all his own hair for a start. Even at the dairy they pulled his leg about being the youngest milko' they'd ever seen, he wouldn't last five minutes according to the old 'un's, but still, he was keen.

"Cup of tea lad?" said Sam as he swung open the top half of the kitchen stable door. The youngster jumped back slightly, not expecting to see anyone up at that time of the morning.

Yes, he would love a cup, thanks, two sugars, and "we'll have the cream off a Jersey Gold-Top to go with it," he added with a grin. He would put the money in later.

Sam frowned a little, he didn't like to think that the boy was pinching the milk, but the lad promised him it was alright: he often drank two or three pints during the course of his daily milk-round and always paid for them after.

Being young he ran for most of it. Rushing up and down people's paths; leaping over garden walls so as not to waken anyone with the opening and closing of creaky gates in the early hours, and the milk kept him going. If he kept up a goodly pace he could do the whole round in six hours. Not bad for nearly six hundred pints to over three hundred homes, he thought. So they settled back and drank their tea complete with its rich golden topping.

Sam was curious as to why the young milkman had come so early, he didn't normally meet anyone at five o'clock in the morning, especially on these cold drab winter days that seemed to go on for ever. Was it that strange feeling he wondered quietly to himself; had the lad woken up this morning and felt it too? He wanted to ask but no sooner had the boy gulped his last mouthful down than he was off. He wanted to push on, something about this morning felt different and he just felt like it wasn't the right thing to do; to just sit around and let it pass you by.

That made up Sam's mind. He knew this day would happen and when it did, he knew it was time to be doing something himself. It was time to move on. He would 'push on' as the lad had put it.

Not that Sam wasn't happy living in the Hostel. He tried to spend each Winter somewhere comfortable and warm. Sleeping out under the stars was fine in the Summer, but when those cold November nights arrived, he knew he should look for something more suitable. His 'winter-quarters' as he always told folk on his travels. 'I'll be off to my winter-quarters' he would say with a soft grin, as though he was one of the landed gentry off to the Continent or somewhere. It always made him smile.

So - it was today. Time to go.

The days were still short and the nights a bit cool to say the least, but when Mother Nature 'wakes you up' you just have to go along with it. Not having many belongings, he was packed quite quickly, giving his little room a quick scan for any forgotten items, and was off. The folk who ran this particular Hostel would be sad to see him leave. He was a friendly old sort who earned his keep by doing odd jobs about the place for them, chopping wood, lighting fires, repairing leaky roofs, that sort of thing, and they'd been more than happy to provide him board and lodgings in return for his services; but even they knew it wouldn't last forever, he would always move on.

He'd stayed with them previously, some three years ago, he had repaired their old Victorian greenhouse for them that time. It was one of those old wooden one's, painted white, and before he'd chanced along it was in a very sorry state. It took him most of that Winter to do it, taking out all the broken panes, replacing rotten timbers, fitting new glass, and finally re-painting the whole thing, but when it was finished everyone was pleased. They gave him a little farewell party that time. Not today though. Sam was content to just slip away quietly as this Winter had been a bit slow. There weren't any major jobs to do, just small things here and there, hardly enough to tax him, and he didn't feel as though he'd really earned his keep this time.

It was still only about eight o'clock as he said his thank-yous and goodbyes to the Staff without any fuss and proffered that 'he might be back this way one day - who knows'. Even Sam himself didn't know, it was like this morning when he woke up. It just suddenly falls into place, it suddenly feels right. You can't argue with Life. If the Almighty had to give reasons for everything He had done, thought Sam, then nothing would have gotten done and none of it would have made any sense. What was the point trying to figure out why the flowers started bursting out all over the place at a particular time each year, you might just as well accept what's happening and sit back and enjoy it. That was Sam's philosophy. Life would take care of him, it always did, and if he could repay it along the way, then so much the better. He never liked getting something for nothing.

As he passed through the huge wrought-iron gates at the entrance to the Hostel he stopped to say cheerio to the gatekeeper and his wife. They'd miss him, thought Jack, as they stood chatting together about the coming Summer. It was handy having another man about the place to help with the upkeep. All those lawns to trim, bushes and hedges to clip. It was a pity they couldn't persuade him to stay a little longer, seeing as how the Season was just starting, and things would start growing hell-for-leather if he didn't keep on top of it. Still, they knew from the past that Sam was a roamer. He would always move on.

They didn't like to think of him as a Tramp. He was always clean and well mannered, and his clothes were presentable enough, probably hand-me-downs from some charity or other but nevertheless clean and tidy. No, they saw him more as a Wanderer, a Loner, a kind of restless soul who has to keep moving on. It was strange really, as they watched him disappear around the bend at the end of their private lane it occurred to them that they didn't really know him at all. They didn't know if he had anyone, any relatives, where he had come from, or indeed where he was going to. They just knew that he was a kindly old gent who had ambled into their lives for a while and now was off again, and that they liked him. And that they'd miss him.

A couple of hours later Sam had made good time and was well clear of the valley which had been his home for the past few months. The Hostel could just be seen nestling between the trees far away behind him in the distance. Hampshire was a genteel county, still quite rural in many places, but the West Country was Sam's favourite part of England. Through Dorset, on to Devon, down into Cornwall, and occasionally up around Bristol and across into Wales. But that was just daydreaming. He had hundreds of miles before him and at his pace, and the way he liked to just meander along all un-purposeful-like, he'd probably not get to Wales again this year. It had taken him so long - nearly all last Summer - to get from Norfolk, down through Constable Country, and into Kent for late summers apple picking, that he'd almost forgotten what it was like to footpad around England like he did. Still, Blandingford was his next choice of somewhere to aim for and he knew from past visits that it was a good couple of days walk from his winter-quarters, so he tried to get a move on.

The days were bright and crisp in the new Spring sunshine, but he knew that the evenings would still be cold. 'A bit nippy' he thought to himself as he pondered on where he would be sleeping for the next couple of nights. It was all very well obeying this strange urge to keep moving on, but he had to be practical and consider his basic needs. At his age he couldn't exactly sleep out in a field in this weather, alright in the Summer when the evenings were long and the night air warm and comforting, but mid-March, not really. So, this was his first task. A bit daunting in some ways, after living like a toff' all Winter in his little staff room at the Hostel.

He often wondered why some of the other staff moaned about their 'poky little rooms'. 'More like prison cells' some would say. Not Sam though, he thought it was like a palace, like living it up in an Hotel, B&B Dinner and All-Found. Not bad reward for a days' work. Still, there was no pleasing some folk. A barn and a bale of hay would be his only respite for the next few months if he was lucky. 'Good enough for the animals, good enough for me' he said to himself as he strolled along.

It was late in the afternoon now and he had spotted a farmer out tending to a flock of sheep a mile or so from the bridleway he had been following and had begun making his way towards him. It was lambing time and Sam knew that any farmer worth his salt would spend hours out in the fields looking after his animals. Bales of hay would not only provide food for the new-born lambs but warmth as well. Once they were a few weeks old they too would not get their farmyard B&B but be out in the fields with their Mum's to fend for themselves, for the time being though they were rounded up every night and shepherded into the barns for warmth. It was no use working all Winter with your expectant flock only to lose some of the new-born to a sudden cold-snap.

Sam waved a friendly hand as he approached the farmer who by now was beginning to make a headcount of his new flock members, so as not to forget any in the rush. That old saying 'follow like sheep' was certainly true, once you could get a leader making her way back to the farm the rest would just follow, like sheep, as it were. The trouble was it wasn't really a one-man job and on this particular day the sight of Sam's smiling face was a sight for sore eyes. It seemed that his usual lad had broken his arm a few days before and yes, 'he could really do with a hand thanks'. Darkness was falling fast and the sooner they got the flock together and bedded down for the night the better.

Sam was a natural with animals, he seemed to have a tranquil manner about him, a kind of inner peace that they could sense and would know instinctively not to be afraid of him. It's surprising how some animals are so nervous when you go near them, sheep in particular nearly always run away when you first walk up to them. Cows on the other hand are so nosy. Stand at the gate of a cow field and they'll lift their heads to take a good long look at you. Hold out a handful of grass and they'll stroll over quite happily for a closer look. Completely dopey really, but as trusting as anything, and yes, up close they really do have lovely big eyes that seem to look straight at you quite knowingly. If only they could talk.

With Sam's affinity and his warm calming nature, they were soon well on their way. Not a big flock, a few hundred head maybe, but enough to contend with for just the two of them. As they made their way through the small meadow and back to the farm the sheep seemed more relaxed and pretty well-behaved. It was just a case of keeping them moving and going in the right direction. With a lull in the proceedings, Sam enquired as to why the farmer didn't have a dog for this kind of work, besides a young lad that is?

"Truth is, I does 'ave a dog, a lovely collie-cross" said the farmer, who by now Sam knew to be called George. "Missy she's called - on account of her bossy nature." He went on to explain that some weeks before she'd been run over at the cross-roads by the farm and the Vet' said she needed plenty of rest. She was alright, no broken bones or anything, but she didn't seem her usual self.

"Probably shook her up," remarked Sam to which George agreed. "I'll have a look at her for you when we get back to the farm, if you like?" It was a sincere offer and seeing the way Sam was with the sheep, patting them, strolling them along, keeping them together effortlessly, George accepted.

George's wife Mollie had seen them both coming as they covered the last few hundred yards towards the farm and had assumed that her husband had managed to enlist the help of someone from the village, wrongly as she would soon find out; and had already begun a huge hot meal for them as by now the Sun had lost all its power and the night was coming in fast. With it the cold air that caught the breath and made hundreds of little sheep nostrils seem to puff merrily in a continuous snort of steam into the night air. The barn was a welcome sight and within minutes the animals were all settled; with fresh food and water they'd be quite content till morning.

That was the trouble with these early Spring days though; morning was a long way off. Winter still had its grip on the land and the days were quite short, Nature couldn't quite make its mind up. The countryside was a-buzz with new life and yet there were more hours of darkness than light, and that meant you had to fit everything you could manage into a 'day' or go without in the 'night'. Roll-on the Summer, lovely light evenings, Sam thought to himself as they walked across the yard and up the path to the farmhouse in virtually complete blackness, and this only about half past five in the afternoon!

Sam didn't actually know what the time was. He'd owned a watch years ago but could never remember to wind it up. It was right at some point in the day and that was fine, but he never knew when that was. He'd have to ask someone the time just to check if his own watch was still working or not. This was ridiculous he decided, and one day while watching some wild brown trout lazily swishing against the current in a small chalk stream, he took it off and threw it in. *Splash!* The fish darted away as fast as lightning setting up a cloud of sediment so as to momentarily obscure the thankless watch from view. With the flowing water rushing by unknowingly the stream soon cleared again like crystal and the trout returned to their game, this time accompanied by a new 'rock' to dance over. Sam laughed as he thought of it, 'someone'll find that one day, all glistening and shiny, and think they've found a secret treasure.'

They'd be right too, for although Sam hadn't realised it, the watch was solid gold, eighteen carat. It had been given to him many years before by a grateful family of old folk, two sisters and their brother, when he'd cut down some overgrown holly trees that were blocking the entrance to their front-door and who for years, unable to do it themselves, had put up with always using the back-door - 'like tradesmen'. Still, he didn't have much concept of wealth, a thing was made to do a certain job and if it didn't then there was no point keeping it. It never occurred to him to sell it or anything, and anyway, it was his own silly fault if he kept forgetting to wind it up, so he should do without and that was the end of it. He often thought he might find that stream again one day and if he did, it would be interesting to see if the watch was still there...

A warm glow from the farmhouse kitchen shone out as Mollie opened the door for them both.

"This is Sam," said George as he gave Mollie a welcome-home kiss on the cheek "he came-along-by earlier, just in the nick of time - don't know what I'd 'ave done wi'out 'im."

It was that soft kind of Hampshire accent, mixed with a little Dorset, which told you that you were in the countryside of Wessex. Not as broad as Devon or 'Zomerzet' but getting that way. Sam felt quite at home. He'd been brought up in Sherborne as a boy, so his own accent was soft and lilting, not quite a country yokel but pleasant to listen to. Being an orphan, you never really knew where to call home as you were sometimes moved around from place to place. In his twenties he spent some time in London which did him no good at all and as soon as he could he moved back to the country.

It didn't worry Sam not knowing his proper background, he was content with his life and 'if he could help someone along the way' as he put it to Mollie, then that was all he asked.

The two men finished their supper with a pleasing jug of mulled ale, brewed by Mollie from last year's hop picking in Kent. She explained that as their farm was quite small, she sometimes supplemented their income by doing other jobs, and for her it was like a holiday.

"Made a nice change," she said, remarking on how lovely it was over there. Sam too had picked hops, but he'd never tried them home brewed before and warmed too.

Next year Mollie was "gonna go back to the cider though - must do somethin' wi'all them apples" she said. She was obviously referring to the small orchard they had passed on their way into the farm which Sam had noticed earlier. It too was all a-buzz with blossom. Another sign to remind him that he was right when he woke up this morning.

Missy was warm and snug by the sitting-room fire when the three of them came in. She lifted her head at the sight of George, wagged her tail softly in recognised welcome and let her head gently rest back down again onto her pillow.

"There - I'm said she weren't right - normally she'd be out'n that basket an' all over us" said George as he patted his faithful old collie and stroked her soft lush coat. She was in good health but there was obviously something not right, Sam could see that for himself.

"I'll take a look at her in the morning, after we've done the sheep, leave her be for now" he said as he too bent down and patted her gently. He could see she didn't really want to be disturbed. Sometimes you can just tell at a glance that an animal is poorly. It's a kind of look that they give you, their eyes go all watery and glistened, as if to say, 'something's wrong - can you help me?' Sam stroked her head gently for a little while longer and as she closed her eyes slowly, he softly lifted his hand away and let her sleep.

Mollie wondered if Sam would like to have a game of cards as they only had a small telly and anyway 'there wasn't much on after about nine o'clock most evenings'. Her and George spent most evenings either playing cards or reading. Country folk seem more content with their lot than most of us. It's not as if you can pop out to the pictures' or go to a show when you live in a small village. Perhaps a pub for a game of darts or table-skittles maybe, but on the whole, you made your own entertainment and anyway, more often than not you had to be up at the crack of dawn, so late nights were unheard of.

They played one or two rounds of Punch, but Sam couldn't quite get the hang of it, he said he was better at the less complicated games - 'Snap for instance,' - which made them both laugh. He was always putting himself down, always had. He never liked anybody to think he was being clever, getting too big for his boots. Truth was, he was quite intelligent, in a worldly-wise kind of way. He'd not been up to much at school, played truant quite a bit, and could never really concentrate. He was always miles away, "daydreaming again Bishop?" as his teacher used to say giving him a clip round the ear as he said it. Even then he always felt as though he wanted to be somewhere else. That's probably why he ended up living the life he did. But living that life taught him more than any school could ever have, it taught him the Lessons of Life itself, and he learnt many lessons.

At George's suggestion he graciously accepted the invitation to sleep the night in the spare bedroom - he protested, (only slightly), that the loft in the small hay-barn would have been plenty good enough for him, but didn't push it too much as this was his first night on the road and he had been living the life of a softy for the past few months. Better to do it in stages, he thought. In the event it was only an old put-up bed in what was not much more than an occasional bedroom cum-storeroom, so he needn't have worried. That night he slept better than for a long-time, the silence of the farmhouse compared to the hustle and bustle of the Hostel was most pleasant, save for the midnight intrusion of Missy jumping up on the bed...

The next morning Sam and George were up and out with the sheep just after six thirty even though it was still fairly dark, the animals themselves were restless and hadn't really like being penned up all night.

"Thankless so-and-so's," mumbled George, as they all seemed to rush at once for the open barn-door "you'd never think all I was trying to do is look after 'em, keep 'em safe." Sam smiled.

Back at the farm Mollie was soon out and about in the early morning sun looking for any fresh-laid eggs. They let a flock of chickens roam about the place scratching a living where they could find it and an old dairy-cow, past her prime but she still gave a few pints a day of rich creamy milk, was allowed to wander about the small meadow. All they needed was a bit of looking after, a bit of corn, some silage from last summer's grass-cutting and they were happy with their lot. At least they were free.

Mollie had heard about this new invention, battery farming, over at the stock-holders market one time, and she'd said then, "George", she said, "I'm not 'avin' my 'ens plugged into no elec-trickery."

He laughed. "You silly old trout - them don't mean that, they's on about a new way of keepin' 'undreds o' hens in a pen so's to get more eggs out'n 'em."

She couldn't see the sense in that, "a hen'll only give you what she wants to, you can't force 'em" she said, "no good'll come of it," and that was the end of that piece of new-fangled technology.

Mind you some mornings she thought it might be an agreeable idea to have all your hens laying in one place, easier to find your eggs that way, instead of anywhere they pleased. In the barn, in the hayloft, in the old tractor shed, out in the scrub, in the hen house even! She would just have to keep on looking.

An hour or so later the unmistakable smell of fried breakfast wafted across the yard as the two men came walking back from the top pasture. Bacon sizzling, eggs frying, tomatoes grilling, sausages sizzling, the kettle whistling, and a great plateful of bread and butter to boot. It fair made them wilt.

Working in the outdoors made for a pretty powerful appetite and Mollie knew they'd be hungry, and she was more than happy to lay on a big spread for the both of them. She didn't see it as being the 'little woman at home', no, on a working farm everyone did their bit. It wasn't divided into men's work and women's work; she could drive the tractor as good as any of them and when they needed extra help in the lambing-sheds, Mollie was in there with the rest. She just felt that if her husband had worked hard all his day's then she should show him her appreciation and give him all the help and attention she could. As well as a little loving along the way of course. A bit of slap and tickle. Like all country-folk, they had no shyness when it came to matters of love. With the way Mother Nature worked, every little bird and bee was a'humming and a'buzzing looking for a mate. Bucks, Rams, Bulls, Roosters - they all strut their stuff when it comes to attracting the ladies and to be on a farm with it all going on around you, well you didn't have much choice but to join in.

Sam noticed how much Mollie and George were in love. It was the way they looked at each other. He'd give her a little wink; she'd smile that girlie smile that had first caught his eye. He'd whisper saucy suggestions in her ear, she'd wiggle her bum at him, and they'd both giggle and laugh at the fun of it all. It was plain to see that they still enjoyed going to bed with each other and with Spring in the air as they say, today was no exception. Sam didn't want to cramp their style so offered to take Missy out for a walk after breakfast and see how she behaved. Mollie smiled at George.

Striding out across the yard and through the farm gates, Sam had decided to follow the roadways with Missy, avoiding the fields on purpose, and because of the obvious danger, he'd put her on the lead. She was a lovely dog, a kind of border-collie mixed with a bit of labrador maybe which gave her a genial manner and made her well-behaved. It was no use having an animal that barked and howled all the time when you were working on a farm, especially working with sheep. You'd have an Alsatian or something if you wanted a noisy guard-dog, but then you couldn't do much else with it. A collie on the other hand was a treasure. They were friendly, likeable, loveable, obedient, and if anyone strange came prowling around in the middle of the night, they'd prick up their ears in an instant to warn you. The slightest noise and they were up.

She seemed a bit nervous walking along the road; perhaps she could still remember getting knocked into by the car a few weeks before but seemed happier being on the lead rather than loose. This was Sam's idea. He'd wondered if she was 'afraid to go out' since being run over, and that was the reason she'd stayed in the house all the time. Maybe she was frightened. It seemed more and more likely that Sam had guessed right for every time a car or lorry went by, she cowered down slightly, not moving, until it had passed. Then when the road was clear, she was bright and happy again. Well, perhaps not exactly happy, but happier.

They had a good couple of hours before it was sheep herding time again and as Sam hadn't been in this area for a few years, they took it at an easy pace. He recalled that there was a small village in these parts, before Blandingford anyhow, and that it was probably the village to which George had referred to last night, 'a drink and a game o' darts in the local pub,' so Sam made his way there.

Arriving in about half an hour Sam realised he had been there before. He'd not stopped that time, just gone straight through, but he had a good memory and recognised some of the shops. The baker's that had been kind to him, letting him have 'yesterday's bread' for a few shillings and the newsagent who had let him have a free read of the papers'. He didn't worry too much about keeping up with the news but every now and then he liked to see what was going on in the world. Keep abreast of things. After all, it was no use him being in a pub somewhere and someone talking about the Prime Minister or someone else famous and him not knowing who it was. That would be daft.

Missy seemed quite at home in the village, a couple of passers-by stopped and patted her, "Hello Missy - where you off to?"

"She's got a day-off today," answered Sam, explaining that she was not feeling herself. "I'm staying at Dappers Farm for a few days and offered to take her for a walk."

Missy seemed to perk up a little at all the attention and Sam could feel her pulling on the lead now and start to walk on with a bit more vigour. She was heading straight for the village pub...

The landlord, a fat faced jolly man with a pickled-red nose and a bald patch where his hair used to be immediately recognised Missy and poured a lemonade-shandy into a bowl and split a packet of potato crisps. She liked to eat them from the bag, holding it down with her front legs in between her paws like a squirrel, so he had to remember to remove the little blue wax-paper bag which contained the salt.

"You 'ave to watch her, she'll eat anything" he said, adding that this was "on the 'ouse seeing as 'ow I 'aven't seen you in nigh on three weeks Missy old girl."

Sam ordered a half of mild and a scotch-egg, that would keep him going till later. As they chatted in the bar, he explained how he was helping out at the farm for a few days while their lad was off. He'd broken his arm in an accident apparently. As it turned out though the two elderly old codgers Sam was chatting with mentioned that he hadn't completely broken it, more of a bad strain really, and laughed. Mind you, it was still in a plaster-cast, but he'd be as right-as-rain in a week, or so they reckoned. Sam was pleased. He would enjoy his stay at the farm, he knew that George and Mollie were lovely people, but he didn't want to be stuck there for weeks on end. He'd only just left the confines of the Hostel and if he was going to get right down to Cornwall by the summer, he had to keep moving on. Talking of which, he reminded himself to ask someone the time, an old habit, and decided it was time they were moving on, back to the farm to lend a hand with George and his sheep gathering.

Missy was a lot better on the way home. The occasional lorry that thundered by still put the wind up her a little, but she was definitely better with the cars. He still had her on the lead, so he had presumed right, she was happier for the moment to be taken control of rather than left to her own devices, like when she was out on the farm.

Coming through the small meadow which looked straight across to the farm they could see George out working on his tractor, un-hitching the hay trailer that he used to drop out fresh feed across the fields for the animals. Sam loosened the collar from Missy's neck, and she was off, running quite fast across to where George was working, him encouraging her with a long trilling whistle through his fingers. Her 'call-sign', smiled Sam to himself. It was clear the dog was a lot better, 'still not one hundred percent' as Sam put it, but better.

"'Ow'd d'ya do it Sam old man" asked George, relieved to see his lovely collie nearly back to full whiz again after so many weeks laid low.

"Tell you tonight over supper - let's put her in the house and I'll fetch them sheep with you in two shakes."

"Of a lamb's tail" said George instantly with a big belly-laugh tagged on. "Of a lamb's tail - 'ow do I think of 'em" he mumbled to himself as he watched Sam walk Missy across the yard and into the house.

"He's happy," Sam said to Mollie as she came to the door.

"Yes," she said with a wistful smile, "been a good day today - been quite nice. See you after."

As she closed the door Sam caught a glimpse into the kitchen, fresh-baked bread laid out on the kitchen table and a big chunk of home-made cheese and pickle by the side. Someone had eaten well at lunchtime he thought, better than his scotch-egg. As he passed by the kitchen window, he noticed something else. Mollie was singing.

"They'd definitely had a good day today," he chuckled to himself "good job I went out." Having read back through his travel journal before leaving the Hostel and thinking about where to go next, Mapleton came back into his mind and he had looked up the entries for Mrs Henderson, Barbara, his 'Devon beauty' as he often called her. It would be nice to see her again as it had been a few years since he'd been back this way.

Fetching the sheep and bringing them back to the safety of the barn again went without a hitch. Sam was a natural.

"You brought up on a farm?" said George as they ambled across the yard, securing the chickens on the way.

"Not exactly," replied Sam, "sort of grew into it since before I started my wanderings."

"Yearn, but you're not one o' them hobo's like they had in America past times" queried George, "you're more like a kindly old English Tramp type of bloke, a Gentleman of the Road; kind of."

"Sort of, I suppose" said Sam, never having given it much thought. He'd always seen himself as a Countryman, a Wayfarer, a Roamer.

"Kind of romantic say's Mollie." Sam blushed a little at the remark. "She reckons you're one of Life's Loner's who don't 'ave no one to worry 'bout 'em and yet you's always ready to worry 'bout others."

"Is that right?"

"Aye - she say's you're 'enigmatic'. Wandering by, coming into people's lives an' then passing out on 'em again - all mysterious like..."

'Enigmatic' thought Sam. He'd never thought of himself as being an enigma before. "Enigmatic?" he repeated back to George with a slight lift in his voice.

"Yep, old lad - enigmatic - mind you, darned if'n I'm sure I knows what it means!" and he laughed out loud, somewhat deflating the grand thoughts in Sam's mind.

"Another bubble burst!" Sam laughed back to George.

By now Mollie was standing with the kitchen door wide open, "'urry up you two, there's gonna be a frost tonight an' I can feel it comin' on already" she called at them, "leave me standing 'ere lettin' all the cold air in - get a shifty on..." The two of them did a mock shuffle of their feet as if to simulate running.

"Better do as she says Sam old lad" said George "in this mood she'll like as clock you one as soon as look at you" and laughed.

She tried to make herself look stern and forthright but with Sam's smiling face and George's silly grin she just burst out laughing and whacked them both across the shoulder blades as they sheepishly ducked by. A playful sort of whack. After all, she had to let them know who was Boss.

She'd prepared a lovely meal for the three of them, honey-roast ham covered in lots of little black clove buds dotted all over in a criss-cross fashion. 'From our own pigs' she added proudly when they saw it coming out of the oven all glistening and crispy. With roast potatoes and apple sauce and some of her own winter carrots and turnips that she still had left in the root-store, it was a meal fit for a king. Well, this was 1958 and rationing wasn't all that long ago. She'd even put something special on for Missy, ox-liver from the butchers in the village - they only had one cow, and she wasn't worth killing just to feed a dog, so she always bought fresh meat for her.

After dinner the crusty bread and block of cheese that Sam had seen earlier came out.

"Finish off with this" she said "like them cheese and crackers do-in's in fancy restaurants - 'cept we 'aven't got no crackers" she added and laughed.

When they had finished George went into the kitchen to make a pot of tea while Mollie and Sam tidied up. As they all worked Sam watched the two of them, giggling, flicking each other, poking each other. It was the playful jostling of a couple happy with each other and very obviously much in love. Probably strange for them having another person in the house, he would move on as soon as it was practical, as soon as the lad was back, as soon as they were able to cope without him.

They sat in quiet silence in the sitting-room with their mugs of tea. Missy curled-up in front of the open log-fire which glowed warmly in the huge stone fireplace; that rich red glow which danced images about the room like a flickering sprite. Occasionally a knothole would spit and fizz as the resin sealed inside it began to boil under the fierce heat of the flames, drawing up the chimney a plume of sweet-smelling apple-wood smoke. From outside the house small sparkles of burning red-hot embers would every so often rise up into the night sky like little twinkling fireflies. Inside the three of them were warm and cosy, not speaking much to start but just slowly unwinding from the day's toils. Sam remembered he was going to explain his theory about Missy but for now decided to leave it. They were all beginning to doze off anyway, so it didn't seem worth it.

The next morning it was raining, that horrible drizzle that seems to get everywhere and looks like thick fog. The sheep still had to be seen to though, so it was business as usual for George and Sam. Mollie made a beef stew with suet dumplings and had it cooking on a slow ring virtually all day. 'They'll be in need of this tonight' she said to herself as she stared out of the kitchen window into the gloomy distance across the yard. She was right too. The dinner that night was most welcome. George wondered if Missy had had a good day today, even though the weather wasn't at its best. Sam answered that she hadn't been too bad considering this was only his second day with her. In the sitting-room after dinner Mollie asked if Sam's theory had proved right and he said she'd been a good dog today and patted Missy softly on her head.

He knew she was technically a bitch being the female variety of the canine animal, but that word had been lost to the vocabulary when it had begun to be used in a derogatory manner as a vulgarity. George and Mollie didn't use the term and neither would Sam. She wasn't a horse or a cow or a pig, each one having its own male-female titles which could be more politely spoken, no; so, she was a lady dog, plain and simple. And in any case, it didn't seem decent to call her a bitch... sounded like you were swearing at her.

He had wondered if Missy wasn't herself because she could remember what had happened to her the last time she went out. A car had gone through the cross-roads, not too fast, but Missy had run out to aim across the paddock and the two had collided. She hadn't been run over as such, more run into. She caught a glancing blow against the side-wing of the car which tossed her back into the verge. She wasn't injured, but as the vet said, she was a bit shook up. So, Sam had reckoned that whenever George took Missy with him across the farm, she wouldn't have been leashed, untethered so-to-speak; normally content to obey her Master and keep by him. That was all well and good normally but with her accident she obviously didn't feel safe going out. By putting her on the lead Sam had taken control, and hey presto! she made it to the village and back on her first day out for ages.

George was amazed. "Daft old girl," he said, patting Missy fondly on her haunches "you should've said you was frightened."

Mollie moaned at him for not thinking of the lead himself. " 'An 'er been sittin' about the 'ouse these past three weeks!"

Sam cut in, not wanting to cause a row between the two of them, "well, not really, it's not the first thing you think of - is it?" They both agreed that they hadn't. "You see, when an animal has complete freedom, like your hens and the cow, they get to thinking they can do as they please. Trouble is with Missy, she's free - and she's not."

Sam went on, "as a sheep-herders dog she has to obey every little twitch of her Master when they're out on the land together." George nodded in agreement. "But when work's finished, she is free then and pretty much does as she pleases, work is over and it's playtime." They both continued to listen, Missy sat right in front of them hogging the fire, completely non-plussed. "So when she ran in front of that car she didn't know what to do, she wasn't injured, but she wasn't fit either."

"So I had to struggle on, on my own" said George.

"Precisely, and as you're her Master she felt she'd let you down but couldn't do anything about it." At this point Missy seemed to sense they were talking about her and quietly looked up.

"Basically, she was afraid of doing anything without you to look after her. By putting the lead on and taking control, I became her new Master temporarily and she was happy. Another few days with her and I think I'll have her confidence back completely."

They were astounded. How could Sam come up with all that after just two days in their company and yet they themselves hadn't had a clue? Surely it couldn't be that simple, that Missy was afraid of going out? Still, there was no denying the change in her, she was definitely more alert and attentive. George gave her a good long pat on her back and stroked her head like he'd always done, and her tail started to wag.

There was something magical about the bond between a man and his dog, almost mystical.

"Well Sam, if you can do this much good in just a couple of days then I reckons you'm 'll 'ave to both go out again tomorrow" said Mollie as she watched her husband fussing over the dog.

"An' the next day an' all" said George softly.

"Fine by me," answered Sam as he stifled a yawn "but for now, I'm off to bed, it's been a long day what with the rain and everything..." They both wished him a good nights' sleep.

"See you in the mornin' Sam old lad," called out George, who turned to Mollie and said quietly "what do you reckon to that then - he must be one o' them animal psycho-mol'o'logists or somethin' - don't you think?" and Mollie nodded.

The next few days passed-by much the same with George and Sam tending to the sheep. Leading them up to the top meadow for a day in the sunlight and then walking them back each evening to the comfort of the barn. It wouldn't be much longer that they would have to keep doing it, as most of the new-born lambs were by now several weeks old and were out of any immediate danger to the vagaries of the weather. Although it was Spring in late March there was still a chance of a cold snap but with each day the new flock got stronger and stronger. Each day Sam would get back after the walk-out, have a cooked breakfast and then take Missy out. She seemed better every day, even coming off the lead when they were on the footpaths through the fields. Wouldn't be long now, she'd be right as nine-pence.

It had been nearly two weeks since he had happened across Dappers Farm. Its inhabitants had all made him very welcome, George had even insisted on giving him some wages - fifteen shillings a week. Despite Sam's friendly refusal he persisted strongly enough for Sam to know that to keep rejecting his generosity would only upset him, so he had graciously accepted. He thought he would give it a few more days with them and then start to think about moving on. After all, he had a long way to go this Summer and he'd barely made a dozen or so miles from the hostel, as the crow- flies. He wouldn't spring it on them though, they were too friendly for that; no, he would wait till the time was right, wait for the right moment, and then he'd tell them.

That evening they watched a bit of television for an hour or so, some play about a Roman Emperor or other, but George had got fed-up with it. "All blinking foreign to me" he said, looking at the papers to see if 'The Army Game' was on.

He liked a good laugh did George. It wasn't. Instead, they sat quietly and talked. Mollie brought up the terrible events of February, all those young footballers losing their lives in that awful aeroplane crash in Germany.

"Munich ..." added Sam quietly.

Yes, that was the place. How upsetting it must have been for all their families. George nodded in silent agreement. Sam remembered he had been scared on a plane once, during the war when his regiment had to drop behind enemy lines. All the while he kept thinking they would be blown-up any minute and was so relieved when they finally jumped and landed with a bump onto terra-firma, even though he should have been more frightened of being shot at! It was something about flying that didn't quite click with him. George reminisced a little about his time in the war, he was a bit too young to have been involved with all of it, just came in at the tail-end. Maybe that's why he liked the Army Game; he could relate to Bootsie and Snudge as he often said to Mollie that he knew blokes just like that in his training barracks.

The next morning Sam decided to fetch Missy with him and George when they went out early with the sheep again, see how she was. George was pleased. He'd missed her company. Mollie was pleased, it meant she wouldn't have to keep worrying about the dog anymore. Sam had worked wonders in the short time he'd been with them. At George's suggestion he took her for a good long walk in the afternoon as well, down through the lower meadow and across into Acres Copse to give her a go chasing rabbits. That night after dinner Sam had a read of the papers, just to keep abreast of the world and its goings-on while Mollie sat quietly darning one of George's socks where he had a 'big tater' gaping through which Mollie said he should have been ashamed of. Suddenly George sat up with a start.

"Let's 'ave a go at the Crossword," he blurted out to the other two "in the paper - give us a pencil Mollie!" and with that he reached across and grabbed the newspaper from Sam's hands with a swift apology for being rude, but he was getting fed-up doing nothing, and anyway, it was a bit of fun.

They liked to do the crosswords, 'made your brains work - you had to stop and think' they both opined to Sam in unison. The thing was, they weren't very good at them. What they did to overcome this problem was to go through all the 'across's' one by one and doing the easy ones. You know, like, laid by a chicken - three letters - starts in an 'e' and ends in a 'g' - that kind of thing. Then they'd do all the 'down's' and very slowly they'd start to fill the squares. Eventually they would run out of the easy clues and would have to make an attempt on the next stage. These were a bit harder. They'd call out what they thought an answer was, see if it 'fitted' and 'fill it in'. This, Sam discovered, was why they used a pencil and not a ball-point pen. If they got any wrong, and invariably they did, especially when it came to the third and final stage, the hardest clues of all, the one's they'd left till the very end, then they could rub them out and have another go.

"Bee-blank-Ay-blank-Kaye-blank-Tee" repeated George, pronouncing each letter phonetically for effect, "six letters - to cover you in bed." They had gained all these unconnected letters simply as a result of getting through their stage one part of the proceedings. "Come on Mollie old girl, you should know this one" grinned George "it's what you likes to pull over to your side when we're in bed together and you're feeling cold."

"It's blanket George and don't be facetious" said Mollie, playfully throwing a cushion at him, "I'm not stupid you know."

"'Ere's one" said George, with an air of superiority "see if you can get it - Tends to the land, looks after animals - six letters - ends in arr" he said pronouncing the letter R all rounded and curly.

Before they could both tutt back at him in unison for thinking that they wouldn't know it was 'Farmer' there came a loud knocking at the kitchen door. As it was only about half past seven it didn't bother them that someone had come calling. They didn't do their usual 'who can that be at this time of the night?' - 'I dunno, I'll open the door an' find out' routine. Still, it was pitch black outside so just as a precaution Mollie put the out-door light on before she opened the back door.

"Oh, it's alright" she called back to the sitting-room "it's only young Raymond."

"Allo Mrs. Ellis" said the gangly youth as he stepped in out of the darkness. A crop of ginger hair, tousled and in need of a good comb, flounced atop his head and hung shaggily about his ears. He was blinking and screwing up his eyes trying to get them adjusted to the brightness of the house lights. As Mollie walked him through into the sitting-room Sam realised his moment had just arrived, courtesy of the five-foot ten-inch string-bean in long trousers and black welly-boots who had just walked into the room.

"Allo Mister George, sir" said the string-bean "I've come to say, me arm's better now, and did you want I back again now?"

"Well, I don't know Raymond my boy" said George, completely taking the puff out of the youngster "see, we got old Sam here who's been 'elping us out these past three or four weeks an' I don't likes to just get rid of 'im, not just like that..." Mollie could see a mischievous glint in George's eye and she could also see the young lad starting to squirm a little.

"Don't let him tease you like that Raymond, of course you can come back, Sam here 'allus said he'd be moving on again soon, and I'm sure 'ee don't mind, do you Sam?"

Sam smiled at the young string-bean, "of course not, I was going to say something this week anyway. I've got a long way to go this Summer, and I can't do for staying here too much longer." This had the immediate effect of putting the smile back on the young lads face and making George laugh out loud at his jolly jape.

"'Ad you goin' there for a minute young Raymond, didn't I?"

"You sure did Mister George, sir - you sure did" replied the boy, "'an me mum 'ould've killed I if'n I 'adn't got me ol' job back, seein' as 'ow it were me own fault about 'urting me arm in the first place."

Sam gave a puzzled look as he had naturally assumed that the boy had injured himself working on the farm.

Mollie explained how the boy had come off his bike in the village square. "Showing off to the girls, riding with no hands, and crashing straight into the Vicar's parked car" she said wagging a disdainful finger at him. They all smiled at the thought of it.

A late-night pot of tea ended Sam's time with George and Mollie Ellis, in the morning he'd be off. The boy was okay now so they wouldn't be needing him anymore. He thanked them for their kindness and generosity and retired to bed. Missy was up to her old strength again, the new-born lambs were well on their way, the chickens were happy, and the cow was showing the benefit of fresh grass in her daily milk yield.

All was well with the World and Sam had a few shillings in his pocket. Tomorrow would be a bright, shiny new day.

Chapter 2

A bivvy for a bed

The lovely thing about being an early riser was that you were up and about when most people were still asleep, so as a consequence you saw the world while it was still fresh and clean. If you've never tried it before you don't really know what you're missing. The dawn rising over the tree-tops or far-away rolling hills is a sight to behold. Early in the morning the industrious to-ing and fro-ing hasn't started, and everything is clean and sparkly. You could be anywhere in our lovely countryside, and it will guarantee to amaze you; to lift you if you're feeling low, to warm you if you're feeling cold. It really was a wondrous, almost religious experience.

Even a rubbish-tip, at the crack of dawn, can look like a kind of urban Stonehenge with the Sun rising up over the horizon and slowly awakening the mighty pile. Smokey steamy vapour clouds rise skyward as the warmth of the day falls on its smelly rotting heaps of waste. The dawn-chorus beginning while it is still dark and gathering in pace with the arrival of daylight: getting louder and louder as more and more birds join in the chain and start their chirruping songs. It's a wonderful moment.

People have to earn a living though and it's not long before the rest of the world around you starts to wake up and the day takes on a completely new persona. Motorcars, lorries, buses, all plying their trade: belisha beacons flashing on and off regulating the flow of pedestrians, traffic lights regulating the flow of vehicles. Shops opening for business; market-stall barkers calling out their wares: children answering the school bell chimes: husbands and fathers answering the factory hooters: and wives and mothers answering to everyone: and all of it coming together as one in the daily routine of a 'day'. Earning a living, getting on with life. This was the reason Sam was a loner. He never felt comfortable with permanent living, all the hustle and bustle was too overpowering. It was also the reason why he kept to the backroads, the byways and the country lanes, the fields and the meadows on his wanderings. He liked to by-pass the big towns as much as possible.

With his years of travelling, he knew his favourite places to aim for and he knew the one's to avoid. So it was that this particular bright sunny morning he'd had a bit of luck. He'd made about fifteen miles over the last few days since leaving the Ellis's - all on foot and at a pleasant regular pace, but he really wanted to be further into Dorset by now and on his way to the coastal-roads.

Up before the Sun as usual he'd walked maybe a quarter of a mile or so from his overnight stop and what should happen along but a milk-lorry. Diesel engines hum and whine as they monotonously drone their cargo along such that even in the early dim of a cold April morning you can hear them coming for miles. Sam had stood to one side of the narrow roadway so as to let the lorry pass by when it got nearer and had turned into the headlights so that he would easily be seen. Being naturally friendly he doffed his somewhat crumpled old hat and gave the driver a cheery early morning smile.

"Morning," he silently mouthed as the lorry came into full view.

To his pleasant surprise the engine slowed and the chuntering, clackety old heap came to a juddering halt. "Mornin' old feller" called out the driver, "does yew want a lift?"

"Wouldn't say no..." replied Sam and in a trice was up in the cab and they were off. The miles flew by, well, as best they could in this clattering old heap.

An hour and a bit later they'd travelled a good twenty or so miles by Sam's reckoning and the lorry was nearing the end of its route. Along the way they'd stopped at various farms to collect the milk churns for the dairy. Pick up full one's today and leave clean empty one's ready for tomorrow. For his gratitude in being given a lift Sam was only too pleased to help out, he never liked getting something for nothing. With the morning sunshine beginning to warm him he'd taken off his old WW2 greatcoat, a heavy great thing, sort of mucky brown coloured, held around the middle by an old leather belt. Ideal on these cold crisp April mornings or at night sleeping in a hay loft, or a make-shift igloo in a hayrick but murderous when you tried to work in them. Talk about work up a sweat. Bill, the driver, had offered him a jug of the new fresh milk but Sam had declined. He'd have something later when they were finished. "Full of calcium is milk..." said Bill as he guzzled a mug-full straight from the churn.

When they reached the dairy, they unloaded the metal canisters of liquid nourishment and neatly stacked them in the cold store. Later today when the cream had settled ready to be skimmed the remaining milk would be emptied into the bottling machinery and bottled-up ready, fresh for tomorrow morning's doorsteps. From the farm to the teacup in twenty-four hours. Gold top: all rich and creamy and lovely in coffee, if you could afford it. Silver top: plain and ordinary, cheap enough to drown your cornflakes in or give to school kids at ten o'clock every morning 'to help build strong teeth and bones'. And finally, Red top: unpasteurized and untainted. Lovely, straight from the cow just as nature intended, if you've got the stomach for that sort of thing. Perfectly alright on the farm if that's what you're used to, if that's what you were brought up with, but disaster if you were a casual drinker, a day-tripper or a tourist. Tummy-bug city if you weren't careful.

But Sam knew this and that's why he had declined earlier even though he was a bit warm at the time and could have done with a refreshing drink to cool him down. On his travels he frequently stopped over at farms, he found the outdoor existence really to his liking and had often drunk milk straight from the cow with no ill effect, but you had to be vigilant. You had to know what cows and who the farmer was to be trusting enough to chance it. Some of the places he'd seen that morning were a bit, how could you say it, dubious. He was suspicious as to their cleanliness and overall care of the liquid milk once it had been given by the herd. It would be perfectly alright once the dairy had heat-treated and bottled it, quite safe, but in its untreated state he didn't fancy it. Bill was alright, he'd probably been doing this route for years and drinking the milk whenever he felt like it so it wouldn't really have a chance to affect him, but Sam didn't want to risk it. As a traveller and roamer, the last thing he would need is a dose of the trots. In fact, any illness was hard to cope with when you were on the road. No, he told Bill he would rather wait and have a lovely cup of tea when they were done, that way he'd have 'something to look forward to'.

The dairy was on the outskirts of town, so Bill had ridden his bike to work as it was a fair way and he and Sam made great use of it getting back. Bill riding as you would, normal like, sitting on the saddle, and Sam standing up behind him with his hands on Bill's shoulders and his legs astride the back wheel, with both feet balanced precariously on the two large three-quarter inch hexagon nuts holding the wheel to the frame. What a pair. Bill, at least in his early forties, and Sam, a somewhere-around-fiftyish if only he could remember what year it was, both careering off down a country lane made of clinker and fly-ash like a couple of twelve-year-old schoolboys.

"Hold on tight Sam old boy" called out Bill as he gamely tried to pedal fast enough to stop the bike wobbling and the both of them falling off.

"Wilco!" shouted Sam back again, desperately hanging on with one hand and trying to keep hold of his hat with the other. Luckily the few belongings Sam did have were all either tied on or stuffed into his rucksack which was slung over his shoulders, so they could take care of themselves. He was more worried about himself... And besides, it would be stupid to go right through a World War unscathed only to come a cropper on the back of a bike by falling ay-over-tee and breaking your neck or something. That wouldn't do.

In the town Bill slowly ground to a halt, his little legs fair shaking with the strain of keeping the bike going at such a fast speed for the last two miles.

Declaring he was 'completely knackered' he led Sam to his favourite caff 'The Tin Plate' for the cup of tea he'd promised him, but he said they'd have to walk the last few hundred yards "cos' he couldn't pedal no more." Sam didn't mind; he was worn out himself just from hanging on. He still had a fair bit of the money left from working at Dappers Farm and as he hadn't had a proper cooked breakfast since leaving George and Mollie, he thought he would treat himself. He also thought he'd better treat Bill, seeing as how he was definitely out of sorts and couldn't wait to sit down, poor old bugger. Billy-can tea and camp-fire poached eggs were fine in their way, but you couldn't beat a good English Breakfast especially when the fried eggs were soft and runny, and the fried bread was crispy and crunchy. The Tin Plate was an uncompromising success and earned itself a mention in Sam's journal.

It was mid-morning now and when they had eaten Bill gave Sam directions as to how to get out of town by crossing the playing-fields and cutting through the woods to the main-road. From there he would only be a few days walk to the coast. Sam couldn't have planned it better if he had tried. Nearly the end of April soon be going into May, lighter evenings and earlier mornings, maybe he might make it to Wales this year after all. He'd had a good start anyway.

That evening he slept in a makeshift. A few bales loosened from a haystack, enough to make a small enclosure, drape his greatcoat over the top for a roof and bobs-your-uncle, a home-made 'igloo'. Warm and cosy with the sweet smell of the straw to send you off to sleep. Mustn't leave it like that in the morning though. If there's one thing that sleeping out had taught him, it was always to pack everything away again before you leave. You shouldn't leave any evidence that you've been there. If he had made free use of someone's belongings - and a haystack in the middle of a field had to belong to someone - then the least he could do was put it all back ship-shape when he'd finished. No use getting a bad name for yourself or folk like you, especially when you might need that bed some other time in the future. No use upsetting people making them feel like they've been rifled or something. People wouldn't take too kindly to that, someone helping themselves to something and not giving something in return, like the effort needed to put everything back where you found it. That was his philosophy anyway. Even tidying up a bit if it was needed. Sam didn't like to get something for nothing, he always felt he had to repay a kindness and as he never had any money to speak of, he repaid it with his own labour. He might be walking through a field and notice a gate with a busted latch or a fence post broken. Ten minutes and a quick knot or two of twine and an instant repair was carried out. What did it cost you? Nothing save your time and your energy. If only more people could be like it thought Sam as he dozed off to the eerie sound of a barn owl screeching far away in the distance like a victim of a werewolf.

He had a restless night. It rained...

Living an outdoor life was wonderful. You pleased yourself; you did what you want whenever you wanted. Trouble was, it was also quite grotty at times. Especially when it was cold and damp, and even more so when it had been raining. Or like this morning for instance, when it was still raining and had done so throughout most of the night.

Having used his coat as a roof it was by now sopping wet, luckily it was fairly waterproof and so he himself was at least dry sitting in the home-made bivvy. He'd have to wait for his coat to dry out though so there was nothing for it but to sit it out. This would be a good time to take stock, check out his rations, have a quick count-up of funds and generally waste a bit of time doing boring things while the rain was coming down. First things first though, get the camp cooker going and put some water on for a cup of tea.

He had one of those clever little meths' stoves, made of pressed tin-plate, circular in shape, about eight inches in diameter with a pattern of holes punched into the metal side wall. In the centre was the fuel container, a kind of metal cup which you poured the liquid into rather like a paraffin heater but in this case methylated spirits. You'd wait for a few minutes and the volume of liquid would be sucked up into the inner lining of the cup through a kind of internal wadding. You couldn't see this wadding, it wasn't that that burnt, not like the wick in a paraffin burner which would smoulder away making fumes and smoke all over the place.

Along the rim of the cup was a row of small holes drilled through into the inner lining whereby the spirit fumes of the meths' could be safely ignited as they escaped into the atmosphere. If you filled it right, about a gill and a half, you could have a good half an hour worth of cooking from one infusion. If it ran out while you were actually using it you couldn't risk refilling it while it was still hot, it would have just ignited the meths' and you'd have gone up in a flash of singed eye-brows without so much as a whisper.

Having said that, Sam had used it for so long - he'd bought it some fifteen years earlier - that he could gauge just about perfectly how much fuel to pour into the cup in relation to how much time he needed for the cookery task in hand. Like this morning, a billy-can of water gathered overnight from the rainfall by leaving his tin outside the camp for the night would need about two shots of fuel. One to soak and one to keep liquid in the bottom of the cup so that as the flames got going the wadding could draw-up more fuel and keep the stove at full tilt for the duration of the boil. It was a bit smelly, methylated spirits, but it was cheap, and a pint bottle lasted for ages. The only drawback was that every time he went into a garage or hardware shop to buy it, they always looked at him kind of funny like. As if he was going to drink the stuff or something.

You couldn't regulate this kind of camp stove at all, fill it, chuck a lighted match in, and whoof! off it went. Flames licked quite briskly up around the sides of your cooking pots eventually making them black with soot, but it didn't half cook quickly. A couple of minutes later and a lovely fresh 'pot' of tea was gently brewing in the boiling billy-can. To put the stove out was easy, you just popped on a metal snuff-cap, shaped to exactly fit the top of the flame-cup and like a candlesnuffer it extinguished the flames by starving them of oxygen. Leave it to cool down, pop the tin lid onto the main circular rim and you were done. What a great little bit of kit. The best three shillings of anyone's money thought Sam as he sat peering out of his make-shift bivvy into the pouring rain with a lovely hot mug of tea, cupped in the palm of his hands for warmth.

INVENTORY: he wrote in his journal thinking it would waste a bit more time if he wrote everything down in some kind of list.

'Rucksack. Camp-stove, meths' and matches. Billy-can mess-tins. A Mirror from a Morris Minor. A Brush and Comb. Spare pair of Boots. Three pairs Woollen Socks. Various oddments of Clothing, Underwear etc. Tin Opener. Scissors. Toothbrush. Knife, fork and spoon. Enamel Mug. Penknife. An old tobacco tin with Medals and Money inside.'

That would do for now, he was getting fed-up having to rummage any deeper into his rucksack. He knew he had a few other odds and sods in there somewhere but couldn't be bothered to keep looking. A ball of string came to mind along with an old photograph of his mum and dad given to him by a nurse at his last children's home. Not much to show for after nearly fifty years, but then he didn't need much. If he couldn't carry it with him then it wasn't worth having. Whatever it was.

Right, next. *RATIONS*:

This was laid out in front of him so everything he had was on show. 'Eggs - five. Bread fresh yesterday morning, a bit stale but alright to make toast with. Dried-milk powder. A quarter of Tea. A bit of sugar.' Not a lot really. He'd have to do some shopping soon or go hungry.

Writing in his journal was a sort of therapy for him. The solitude of his life was somehow eased by remembering where he had been in past times, looking back through the pages would cheer him no end. Strolling around the countryside as he did, he would often come across the gypsy fairs in small towns and villages. You could amble around the stalls looking for bargains, watch the horse dealers auctioning their stock, be entertained by the side-shows and jesters, have a few glasses of home-brewed hooch and generally have a jolly time. This year he was hoping to come across one of the bigger Dorset Fairs before the summer came on strong as he was of a mind to get himself a new pair of trousers. Well, old, second-hand, 'new trousers'. He'd kept back a little pot of money for the purpose. Sometimes if he didn't happen to have any cash he would try and barter with the gypsy sellers for the things he needed. He got his latest rucksack and mess-tins like that one year.

He'd always had an old kitbag for his belongings, you know, with a draw-string to pull on as you slung it over your shoulder, but it wasn't easy to carry with all his junk inside and was getting a bit worse-for-wear and this particular fair he'd spotted a stall-holder with a whole array of ex-Army clobber. Tins, knives, boots, helmets, empty bullet cases, shell cases, bayonets, you name it, he had it. He also had a half-a-dozen of those dark green canvas rucksacks with brass buckles and pockets everywhere for putting things in.

"How much for one of them?" he asked the gypsy.

"Ten bob." This was beyond Sam, he had a little money but wanted to keep it back for emergencies, like medicine if he ever got ill. "Sorry," he replied, "but I can only spare five shillings. How much will you give me for this kitbag?" and held out his old grey Army one which was a bit cheeky considering the state it was in, but it was worth a try.

"Two shillings" came the gypsy's reply, who by now had noticed that Sam wasn't a 'regular' from the nearby village. In fact, he looked, in appearance anyway, a bit like a gypsy himself. A kind of kindred spirit. He gave Sam a smile and beckoned him to one side. "Come back later my old mucker and we'll see what we can do."

Sam was taken with his friendliness and promised faithfully to call back at six after the fair had closed. It was worth the wait. The gypsy gave him the rucksack, a set of mess-tins and a brass compass that Sam had been admiring lying atop an old tin box and only asked for the kitbag and the five shillings in return. "Surely not," said Sam, "I can't take all of this from you..."

"You bide your tongue old 'un," said the gypsy, "you're one of us, we can tell" and he put his hand out in a friendly gesture "shake on it and we're done, no arguments." Sam leaned forward and shook the gypsy's hand vigorously "well I don't know what to say."

"Don't say anything," replied the gypsy, "you be on your way now; cushty-bok."

Sam bade him farewell and left. He couldn't believe it. So many people thought of gypsies' as liars and scoundrels, wandering about the country nicking things wherever they went, how wrong they were. He'd always found them charming people to be with and while it was true they were experts at wheeler-dealing and a bit shady at times to say the least, this latest episode just confirmed his own feelings towards them as decent ordinary folk who happened to live a different lifestyle to the rest of us. As he himself did. Perhaps a little rough around the edges but all-in-all hard-working folk with deep rooted family morals and an empathic feeling for all the things around them.

The rain had carried on all day so there was nothing for it but to sit it out. It gave Sam the opportunity to bring his travelling journal up to date. Everywhere he went he liked to keep little notes about his experiences. Reminders of good places to call, references of places to avoid. 'We don't take no beggars and hawkers here' was a phrase that warranted special remembrance.

He abbreviated it to N.B.H. and if he saw that in his notes then he knew not to make the same mistake twice. If he'd received a particularly rude or abrasive rebuff somewhere then he would leave a tell-tale chalk mark on a gatepost or garden wall, warning the next traveller to stay away. It was a kind of anonymous sign language. Folk like him wandering up and down the countryside were not always greeted with smiling faces so there was a secret code of markings and drawings telling the next walker what to expect. There were plenty of agreeable places to stop and as a consequence there was a whole repertoire of signs to denote this. Very friendly. Hot drink given. Cold drink given. Fresh water available. Work. Food. Clothes. Shoes. All sorts of things were covered, each one having its own sign. It was amazing what some people were happy to give. On a hot day you could get a lovely cool glass of barley water, on a cold day a steaming hot cup of tea, or a mug of cocoa if it was even-time. At the local vicarage you could often get a meal or be given a little food to take with you. Sometimes you'd be offered some clothing from the jumble sale collections; shirts, vests, trousers, overcoats that sort of thing.

When a husband died the bereaved widow would usually ask the Church to dispose of his wardrobe, shoes, shaving brushes and so on, and these were then passed along to the needy. People like Sam. He was never going to have enough money to buy all his own things, so these hand-outs were greatly appreciated. When he did earn any money odd-jobbing, then he would use it only when necessary to buy something particular - to replenish his food supplies or to have the odd treat, like the cooked breakfast he'd had yesterday. Which he was now dreaming about as he tucked into two of his remaining eggs, poached as usual in the billy-can. No ketchup today which was a shame, it went so well with eggs. 'Can't stay here tomorrow' he said to himself, 'have to get on - rain or no rain' he continued 'the old coat will just have to be alright.'

He often talked to himself. Well, strictly speaking, not to himself, more to the open air around him. Like now, sitting in his makeshift eating poached eggs for tea with dry toast because he had no butter to put on it and peering out into the rain. 'It'll have to stop soon' he said to an invisible nobody two or three feet in front of him 'or I don't know what'll happen.'

As it happened it stopped soon after but as it was getting dark there was nothing for it but to settle down for the night and get going again first thing in the morning. He'd set off good and early, before dawn, so as to catch up on his lost day. 'Soon be at the coast' he mumbled to himself, trying to keep his somewhat dampened spirits up.

Chapter 3

Lady Felicity

Doesn't it sometimes feel that some things in life seem to be perpetually unattainable. Doesn't matter how much you try, how hard you work, how much effort you expend, they always seem to be just beyond your reach. Like winning the pools, hardly a cat in hell's chance of getting all eight from ten but never mind, you have to keep on trying. Sam's goal was to get across the Peele Valley and up to the top of Henn Point before nightfall. Not much to hope for. He could see it away in the distance. Trouble was no matter how much he kept walking onwards, that distance didn't seem to be getting any shorter. The Point looked as far away now as it had done first thing this morning.

He had made good time in the last two days since his extended overnight rain- stop but determined though he was he didn't seem to be making much headway. It was only the sheer scale of the valley doing this to him of course and although he knew this it didn't make him feel any better. He knew that from the top of the Point you could turn in all four directions of the compass and see for miles. The sweeping vista of downland countryside to the North; Kent and Sussex to the East; Devon to the West and The Channel to the South. Incredible. He'd stood on the top of Henn Point before and witnessed this sight. It never failed to move him. All the effort needed to get to the top was rewarded tenfold with the exhilaration of actually making the achievement, and the bonus was the spectacular view, which was worth it in itself. Sam knew that once he could see the Channel it was only a matter of walking down the soft grass covered southerly slopes of the Henn Headland and he'd be on the way to some of his most favourite countryside. A few hours at most. Thing was, he hadn't even got up this side yet and the outlook across the valley still didn't seem to be getting any smaller.

"Come on you old bugger" he said to the thin air in front of him. "If them cows can do it, so can you."

In the field next door, a herd of bemused Friesians stared at him as he passed by. They weren't used to seeing many people crossing through their meadows. The farmer of course, and maybe the odd walker, but not much more than that. Inquisitive as ever a small group of them started to troop along their side of the fence so as to keep a parallel pace with him. He had to laugh; it was as if they were playing 'follow my leader' with him.

"Silly old ---" he was about to say something unkind but thought better of it and silenced his voice, "no - not really my old dears" he called out to them. Don't want to hurt their feelings, calling them names: you never know, it might put them off their milk. Cows must have feelings too, he thought. They followed like this as far as they were able to. The edge of their field bordered the small river, the Peele, which meandered all along the floor of the valley, so he had to say goodbye. He gave them a cheery wave and 'mooed' out loudly to them as he made his way along the bank of the river to a place where he remembered he could cross.

From his past travels he knew that somewhere along the valley were the remains of an old cobblestone bridge. It had four spans to it originally and was easily wide enough for a horse and cart to cross over and was obviously built at a time when the river was a lot grander. Probably a fairly important rivulet or a tributary of the mighty Charne, but now it was nothing more than a trickle by comparison, not much more than a big stream, as when he reached the bridge the water flow was amiably travelling through a single arch without any cares or worries for the loss of its former glory. It had probably flowed for centuries quite happily and for all anyone knew it was the very river that cut this wondrous swathe through the Dorset hills, all those millions of years ago and laid down the beautiful landscape of the Peele Valley which even now was stretching before him. One day it would be big again but for now it wasn't bothered - it could wait.

Sam decided that as there were only a couple of hours now before darkness he might as well stop for the night here and savour the moment, no use rushing. The Headland wasn't going anywhere, it would still be there in the morning. With the soft grassy banks and a spare arch or two to sleep under for the night the only thing he needed was fresh water and something to eat to complete the picture. Both were immediately at hand, right there in front of him. Fresh sparkling crystal-clear water filtered down through the surrounding chalk hills and fed the Peele River. Wild brown trout, about nine or ten inches long, danced about lazily in its shallows.

Probably all of six inches deep; close enough that with a little patience he could tickle a couple out with ease, well one anyway, and that would be plenty. He wasn't a greedy man; one would be fine for him. He'd managed on just a few wild berries and some field mushrooms with his remaining eggs over the last forty-eight hours so he relished the thought of a freshly cooked trout supper...

The pleasure of spending the night near fresh running water had an added bonus, besides the obvious of food and so on. It meant he could have a good wash and thorough clean up. Pots and pans, socks and underwear, vests and shirts, anything and everything, and of course, himself... The pots and pans were easy, just string them up and lay them in the water-flow. Let the river wash them for you overnight, they'd be spotless in the morning. The clothing was fairly easy, find a couple of flat boulders worn smooth by the incessant flow and bash away, like the natives along the Nile. Hang it out to dry on a nearby fence or in the branches of a tree, fine. But yourself, that was a bit trickier. Imagine - you'd probably be half-naked, sitting on the banks of some stream, trying to clean yourself with the last remains of a coal-tar soap bar; wash your hair, have a shave, that sort of thing, then along comes a troop of Girl Guides or something - charming.

Sam's answer was simple. Wake up even earlier than usual, hopefully hours before the rest of the world, and get all your ablutions over and done with as soon as possible. Put your clean dry clothes back on and no one would know the difference. Simple that is except for one thing, fresh flowing river and stream water was generally freezing, even in high summer, so it was always too cold early in the morning even if the sun came out, so there was nothing for it but to take your chances and hope that there weren't any unexpected onlookers to happen by. And, also, not to hang around too long either, especially when it came to the delicate bits. Mind you, you didn't see many people out and about in the open countryside so you could sometimes take your time and enjoy the situation. Rejuvenate yourself with the invigorating sensation of the sparkling water gushing over you like a torrent. Wonderful.

It was a warm evening and there was still a little time before nightfall, so Sam took the opportunity and stripped off.

Supper was lovely. Trout grilled over the hot embers of a real campfire, with fresh watercress picked from a nearby brook that ran into the river. He didn't feel it right to cook the fish over the meths' stove, you wouldn't get that rich aromatic flavour that the smoke would have imparted to it otherwise. It didn't bother him that a few moments before it had been swimming about, he had been through a world war so there wasn't much that bothered him, except cruelty perhaps. If God hadn't put the food and the creatures of this Earth in all the strange places that he did, then farmers and fishermen wouldn't have had to toil the way they did for their harvests. The animals of the land, the fish of the sea, and the fruits of the Earth. Everything owed something to something else. Everything had to be worked for, nothing was for free. The toil of the job was the work of life, and life was the gift of God, one went with the other. Sam accepted that without question, and hopefully his toils and tribulations would be rewarded. He slept well.

The next morning, he finished off the last of his bread - toasted again as it was quite stale - as he waited for the billycan to boil. His tea supply was getting a bit low, and his dried milk wouldn't last long so he knew he had to be up and over Henn Point headland in the day. He knew he'd have to be down the other side into Hurleston village before any of the shops closed, otherwise he would run out of his essential rations. 'Don't mind not eating for a day or so,' he mumbled as he tried not to burn his toast 'but a cup of tea is a must.'

He still had his emergency-money hidden in the old tobacco tin in his rucksack so he knew he was okay to pay for the supplies, he wouldn't have to beg. All he needed was to make sure he could get up and over the Point in good time so he could actually buy them before the shops shut. And he was really looking forward to having some real milk for a change. And some butter.

The sun was coming up earlier and earlier every day now as the weeks rolled by toward the Summer so this morning it was quite pleasant to be able to sit quietly for a few minutes eating breakfast and just take everything in. This was a lovely spot. The grassy meadows, the refreshing life-giving river, the lovely old, cobbled bridge, the marsh curlew's singing their peewit-peewit song all around him, a distant peel of church bells sounding out matins'. Bunting's singing out their funny little song 'a little piece of bread and no cheeeeese... a little piece of bread and no cheeeeese...' Sam could easily spend several days here he thought as he drifted off into a day-dream sitting on the bank-side with the warm sun on his face and the soft trickling sound of the water gently lulling him off, but as always he knew he had to get on. On the other side of the Point lay Hurleston and that marked the beginning of his journey along the coastal paths and foot-ways through the remains of Dorset, on to Devon and hopefully as far down as Cornwall. Wales didn't seem to be calling him so much now, he didn't feel like rushing through the Summer anymore just to get there as he was beginning to be reminded how much he liked this part of the country. The gentle feeling of contentment that was slowly washing over him as he walked could not be bettered.

A couple of hours later Sam had reached the topmost part of the headland. He stopped for a breather and a drink of water. It was quite warm now, so he was glad of the rest. Looking back, the river and the bridge seemed quite small now. Ever looking onwards, he stood up and began to make his way across the top of the headland. It was kind of flat like a plateau, about a mile each way and criss-crossed with footworn pathways marked over many years by animals, sheep and the like, who roamed about quite freely up here. At the edges the grass just stopped and gave way to dramatic cliffs of sheer sandstone where every now and then another chunk would suddenly rumble and fall dramatically into the sea below. He could see Westward for miles, all hazy in the morning sunshine and it seemed to spur him on, put a little lick into his stride. He'd stop for a proper rest and a brew-up on the far westerly level, just before the grassy slopes of the downward stretch and then it would be a leisurely stroll to the bottom and into the village.

This side of the headland was quite gently sloped as it ran down to the lowlands below so Sam knew he could make it with ease. A cup of tea would keep him going just right. "Hell-oh-oh... - Is anybody there? Hell-oh-oh...- I say, can you help me." Sam nearly spilt his tea! He was miles from anywhere sitting on the top of Henn Point, a pretty bleak and windswept place at the best of times, and someone was calling out to him. Well maybe not specifically to him but to generally anybody within hearing distance. He scanned his eyes around-a-bouts and couldn't see anyone.

"Where are you?" he called out, "I can't see you..."

"I'm over here - just below a big hawthorn scrub - by the cliff-side of the footpath" came the reply. Sam could see the large straggly clump of bushes just fifty or so yards away and rushed over. "Oh, thank goodness..." said the young woman as she saw Sam's figure appear to the side. "I was beginning to think no one would hear me."

"What's the trouble Miss?" asked Sam as softly as he could. She was obviously distressed, and he didn't want to upset her any more than necessary.

"Something darted out in front of the blasted dog - a rabbit or some such - he's gone after it - stupid animal nearly tore my arm off - and in the fraças I've gone and put my leg out down some blasted hole or other." Despite her angry bravado it was obvious she was in a good deal of pain. Maybe this was her way of dealing with it but it wasn't fooling Sam.

"Let's take a look." She looked at him coldly.

"Have you got clean hands?" he showed her his upturned palms, "and the other side." He turned them over, thinking to himself how it was a bit of luck he'd had a good wash earlier. "I suppose they'll do," she said. "At least your fingernails aren't all bitten and chewed - I can't stand bitten and chewed fingernails - it's so common." He gently undid her shoelace and slipped her foot out of her boot, feeling around her ankle delicately. "Careful!" she winced as his fingers felt around her swollen foot, "that bloody well hurts!!"

He looked at her sternly. "For someone so well-spoken you've got a squalid tongue on you Missy" he said.

"I don't know what you mean" she snapped back angrily. "I'll speak how I damn well like. Do you know who I am?" she asked all indignantly. Sam didn't - and he didn't really want to find out, so he just shook his head. "I am Lady Felicity Hurley. My father is Lord Hurley. We own Hurleston Manor."

Sam knew of it. It was the big manor house that dominated the village which bore its name at the foot of the Headland. He'd called there once before on his travels and been given short thrift, although the cook gave him some cold meat leftovers he recalled. It still warranted a broken circle and two lines of chalk on their gate post though, just to warn others. "Well, that's as maybe" he said quietly back to her, trying not to get angry "in the meantime let me finish checking this foot out." She sat silently staring away into space, anywhere but towards Sam. She didn't want to come face to face with him again even though he was doing his best to help her. "Right my dear, I'm afraid you've broken your ankle. There's not much we can do up here so, somehow, we're going to have to get you down into the village where it can be looked at properly" he said calmly. "I'll see if I can scout around and find something to make a crutch of some kind."

"Don't be long" she called out sharply after him, "I've been here for two hours as it is."

'Don't you worry' he mumbled to himself under his breath 'the sooner I'm done here the better.' He didn't really hold out much hope of finding anything suitable for a crutch, the headland was sparsely covered in just clumps of bracken. Old straggly dog-wood roses, blackberry thorns, gorse bushes, nothing substantial enough to take her Ladyship's weight. The odd tree would have helped, he might have found a loose branch to break free, but up here on the top of the Point there were none. After a while he made his way back to her.

"Well, you certainly took your time!" Yes, and good afternoon to you too he thought to himself.

"Sorry about that my Lady, but I couldn't find anything suitable to use as a crutch, so -"

She interrupted him, "well what are we going to do then?"

"As I was about to say - so we'll just have to manage the best we can and that I'll give you a piggy-back."

She stared at him in sheer disbelief. "You most certainly will not - you smelly tramp you - I might catch something..."

"Well, it'll be dark soon and you can't stay here" he replied.

"You walk down into the village" she said, "and I'll stay here."

"Yes..?"

"And then you can bring some help. Fetch some of my father's men to come back with you."

"Fine - and in the two hours that it takes for me to do all this you'll probably pass-out from the pain and exhaustion or something and I'll not hear the last of it from your family for leaving you up here all alone to fend for yourself."

She was taken aback by Sam's forcefulness. "I'm sorry my Lady if I don't meet with your approval - but I'm all you've got. Now - I'm going to gather up all my belongings over there on the ridge and then we're going to see about getting you down this hillside."

"It's a headland," she half-heartedly snapped back at him, trying to keep the upper hand.

"Same difference" said Sam completely nonchalant and turned away to go and gather his things. A lovely fresh brew was still sitting on top of his stove, the last of his rations, stone cold. In the rush he'd forgotten all about it. Oh well...

She was in a fair bit of pain was Lady Felicity and was thankful of Sam's intervention, although she wasn't about to admit it. "I could have managed" she said stubbornly. "Maybe so Miss, but it's quite a long way down and I couldn't see you struggle all on your own."

She was a good-looking young woman, in her early twenties and obviously used to getting her own way, daughter of the Lord of the Manor and all that, so when she insisted that Sam wasn't 'in his wildest dreams' ever going to give her something so common as a 'piggy-back' he hadn't pushed it. At least she accepted his compromise and was using his broad shoulders to lean on as they walked. Smelly or not she had to concur he was right. She'd already laid there for hours waiting for someone to come along and if this scruffy old tramp with a crumpled hat and a straggly beard was all there was, then so be it. She could always have a bath and a new set of clothes when they got to the Manor, so it wasn't too bad. It was slow going and in the last of the afternoon sun, quite warm. He'd managed to tie his greatcoat through the loops on his rucksack, like a bedroll, so that made him a bit cooler but with the weight of his pack on one side and her Ladyship on the other he was soon longing for the lovely cool stream that he'd left back on the other side of the Point.

"We'll stop here for a rest your Ladyship" he said. "You sit over here on this tussock, and I'll fetch you some water out of my rucksack." She was grateful for the stop. Her ankle was by now quite swollen. She'd not managed to put her shoe back on after Sam had removed it and with the sudden release of pressure it had blown up within minutes.

"That's very kind of you" she said, without meaning a word of it. The water was slightly warm having been in Sam's bag all day but never-the-less it was quite welcoming. "Very refreshing" she said as she drank from Sam's old tin mug.

"What are you going to drink out of?" The bottle... he could hear himself wanting to say just to wind her up. "Oh, it's alright" he said, "I've got a billy-can in here, it'll do just fine."

She looked visibly relieved. Can't be doing with catching the 'pox or something from some dirty old tramp you could see her thinking. Sam didn't have the heart to tell her where the water came from, although he wanted to, just to see her reaction. Imagine, a mile or two up-stream and some old cow or sheepdog might have widdled in that river, who would know? I mean, some dirty old tramp might even have washed himself in it for goodness sake. Drink filthy old river water! Never!!

Poor thing, she'd have apoplexy if she knew.

"What are you grinning at?" her Ladyship snapped - waking him from his day-dream – "if you're laughing at me, I'll jolly well - " this time Sam interrupted her.

"Right my Lady - let's be having you - won't be long now, an hour at most - and we'll have you back home before you can say 'lookout it's Andrew Miller'" and with that he stood up, took her arm and gestured for her to move off.

"I thought it was 'Jack Robinson'?"

"Ah well see, there you go, you never can tell these days..." he left it at that. She looked suitably perplexed which made him smile, he'd got one up on her at last.

"Andrew Miller" he said, some twenty minutes later "was a Navy lieutenant in the 18th Century press-gangs who became notorious for his success in 'acquiring' new recruits." He spoke the words to her as though he was reading them from a book, all matter of fact like.

"Really."

"Yes, that's why many old sailors still refer to the Navy as the Andrew" he added, all knowingly.

"I see" she said, not very impressed now that she knew the answer, "I'll have to remember that little gem next time I'm having people over for a dinner-party."

Hmmm, one up to her Ladyship thought Sam.

They didn't speak much after that. There didn't seem any point. She had no interest in what he had to say, and he couldn't be bothered to waste his breath making polite conversation with her anymore. Gentlemanly as ever though he gave her the benefit of the doubt and put her haughtiness down to the pain from her injury, that it was this which was making her facetious.

The sun had slowly dipped westwards over the horizon and the early dull darkness of twilight was taking over the land. A beautiful red hue stretched right across the sky tingeing the clouds with a fiery red brightness that slowly faded into a soft orange glow. Suddenly it wasn't easy to see into the shadows or exactly where you were walking, so it was with great relief that a streetlamp flickered into life on the road just ahead of them. They had made it. One by one the streetlights blinked into life in a random pattern here and there across the village. All their little dusk-till-dawn sunlight detectors, realising that there were no longer any rays falling onto their photocells, flicking over and allowing the current into the bulbs. It wasn't fully dark yet but those shiny beacons with their pool of soft yellow light were most comforting.

The Manor House was only a few hundred yards now and it too was lit up against the all enveloping darkness of nightfall. Lights on in almost every room it seemed to Sam: their bills must be frightening... As he rang the entrance-bell Lady Felicity suddenly went limp, she'd only just made it he thought to himself, she must have been hanging on as long as she could. The door was opened by a policeman, Constable Page the village bobby, who immediately took the other side of her Ladyship and helped Sam to walk her through the hallway into the house. In the Drawing Room Lord and Lady Hurley rushed to their injured daughter, who was by now so limp and weak looking that Sam thought she was about to pass-out.

"Fetch Dr. Clarke" called out a voice. "Fetch me a brandy" called another. "Someone fetch a blanket" came another. "Oh, my darling Fliss, what happened to you?" "We've been so worried." "What on earth have you been up to?" A multitude of voices were ringing out all at once from the gathered throng.

For a few minutes Sam just stood there in the hallway all agog. It seemed like hysterical pandemonium had suddenly gripped everybody, all at once, all at the same time. The Doctor arrived and dashed straight past Sam without a blink. For goodness sake, she'd only broken her ankle, he thought to himself, the way they were carrying on you would think she'd had her arm chopped off in a threshing machine or something! Talk about playing to a crowd. Lady Felicity was lapping it up. Miss High and Mighty 1958 was in her element. All soppy and feeble she lay there on the couch with the pain that was etched across her face being held back just enough for the audience to make remarks such as 'she's being terribly brave' and 'poor thing' and 'Fliss my darling - hold on!' Sam couldn't take anymore, he decided to leave before cracking-up completely at how pathetic it all was. As he made his way down along the huge oak-panelled hallway and out into the darkness he heard the sound of footsteps coming up behind him across the gravel driveway, he turned, it was his Lordship. A kindly looking old soul with goodness in his eyes, about seventy years old.

"I say - are you the tramp chappie who found my daughter?"

"Yes, your Lordship" answered Sam, involuntarily tapping the brim of his hat in acknowledgement.

As he drew closer Lord Hurley lowered his voice. "Don't suppose she's thanked you for coming to the rescue, has she -" he paused.

Sam shook his head, "no matter your Lordship, only too pleased to help."

“Well look here my good man, I know my daughter can be a bit – well…” bad mannered is what Sam wanted to say but managed to hold himself back, “a bit difficult?”

“Well yes, quite, and I know she doesn't always mind her P's and Q's but she doesn't mean anything by it.”

“That's quite alright your Lordship, think no more of it” replied Sam, turning to leave, “I'll bid you a farewell and be off.”

“Wait, before you go, look I know my daughter wouldn't approve, so keep this to yourself, but take this with my best wishes and my thanks.”

He handed Sam a five-pound note. “No, I couldn't - really it was nothing, anyone else would have done the same” protested Sam.

“I'll not take 'no' for an answer. Now you keep it with my blessings and remember, say nothing to anyone” and with that the old boy turned and walked back into the house. As he shut the door Sam found himself silhouetted against the tree-lined driveway by the glare from the house lights blazing away behind him.

As he moved to walk away a thought occurred to him. 'I wonder what time it is?'

With a fiver in his pocket and no shops open to spend it in Sam headed for the village pub. The Crooked Arrow. He'd been there before and remembered that they had made him most welcome, and they did a lovely steak and kidney pie with mashed potatoes and onion gravy. He could even afford to stay in one of their rooms for the night with his reward money, so some good had come out of it, even though he was miffed about not getting his fresh rations on time.

About half past nine he was sitting playing cards with some of the old timers in the bar when PC Page came in. No one took much notice and carried on playing as the young bobby walked over to the bar and quietly chatted to the Landlord. A few minutes later he approached the table where Sam and the others were sitting.

"Excuse me Sir - can I have a word?"

Sam looked up. "What's up lad?"

"I'd rather not say in present company Sir" he replied somewhat officiously.

"I've got nothing to hide Constable - these people know me of old - anything you've got to say to me, you can say in front of them" said Sam quite happily.

"Well Sir, it seems that Lady Felicity's purse is missing with twenty pounds in it - and as you're the only one who's been with her all day today - she thinks you've stolen it..." The young policeman looked quite serious as he spoke, so Sam thought it best not to laugh.

"Well, I don't know where she got that idea from" he said with a look of complete bewilderment. "I've never stolen anything in my life!"

"Can you explain then how come you've booked a room here for the night when, forgive me for saying, but you don't look like you've got two ha'pennies to rub together, Sir."

"I'm sorry my young friend - but I can't" replied Sam and he carried on dealing his cards. "According to the Landlord you've even had a cooked meal tonight and several pints of mild, for which you've paid for all of it with a crisp new five-pound note."

"Very true."

"And you can't tell me where it came from?"

"No, constable, I'm afraid I can't."

"Then you'll have to come with me Sir" announced the young policeman, pointing with his hand towards the door. Sam rose from the table, drank the last few mouthfuls of his beer and turned to the Landlord and calmly said "cancel the room mine-host, I'm sleeping for free this evening courtesy of Her Majesty's Constabulary" and with that he followed the young policeman out.

The group of players sitting at the table clapped and cheered at Sam's jocularity making PC Page blush. They did indeed know him of old and knew very well that his honesty and integrity were beyond reproach. He might not have looked like everyone's idea of a trustworthy person but beneath the crumpled hat, straggly beard and lumpy old greatcoat was a warm-hearted soul who wouldn't do anyone an injustice. Little did they know it was this very integrity that was even now committing him to a night in the cells. Still, he didn't mind, it would save him the cost of sleeping at the pub.

The next morning Sam woke at five am. as usual. For a minute he forgot where he was and had imagined himself back at the hostel then in an instant he remembered. There'd be no early morning trip to the kitchen for a cuppa', he was locked in. Locked in in a police cell. Well, a sort of room in the cellar of the village policeman's tied-house, but locked-in never-the-less. There'd be nothing for it but to wait till someone stirred upstairs. He didn't have to wait long. PC Page, the young bobby who had arrested Sam the night before came in with a piping hot mug of tea.

“I put two sugars in, hope that'll be okay” he said with a bright cheery smile. He'd clearly only just got up as his hair had that bit at the back sticking up in the air where he'd slept on it and his braces were hanging down round his waist. Without his police jacket and helmet on he looked quite young but at least he had his priorities right.

“That'll do just fine lad.”

“I been thinking” the young copper announced as he sat there sipping his own mug of tea, “As how it would be daft of someone to pinch something off someone and then land themselves in it by going with that someone straight into the lion’s den - as it were - by carrying that certain someone straight into the arms of all her friends and family - ” he paused, looking at Sam who was listening intently with a wry smile on his face. “And then to go off all brazen like into the nearest pub as bold as you like, spending for all to see, well it seems to me that a person wouldn't do it.” Sam nodded. “Anyway, I was having a word with the folk in the pub late last night and they reckons you're as straight as a die.”

“Good to hear it” remarked Sam.

“So, I thought I'd get up smart and early this morning and take me off for walk up the Henn and see if I can't find some answers.”

About a quarter to eight the door to the cell opened again and in walked PC Page's young wife carrying a tea-tray on which Sam could see a brimming plateful of sizzling hot food. “My name's Brenda” she said pleasantly, “I thought you might like to have some breakfast with us. Rory's gone off without his so there's plenty to go round.”

Sam accepted without hesitation and started to tuck in, there was nothing he liked better than a big, cooked breakfast, start you off for the day just right and could keep you going till tea-time, lovely "very kind of you young lass."

She sat with Sam for several hours chatting and laughing. She'd said to her husband how he didn't seem the sort to steal, how he had 'honest eyes' and how she could always judge a person by the look in their eyes. As they talked the time flew by. She'd even brought him down some tea and biscuits about mid-morning. 'Elevenses' she said and apologised to Sam as to how she couldn't let him come upstairs into the kitchen really, but she felt she couldn't lock him in either so if he wouldn't mind just sitting there, she'd fetch some more digestives down in a minute. Sam didn't mind, he was getting looked after quite handsomely and it made a pleasant change. It was putting him behind a little on his journey but that didn't matter, he was in no hurry to get anywhere in particular, and anyway, he'd had free board and lodgings for the night so he couldn't complain. He knew he was innocent so what was the odds worrying about it, Lady Felicity - Fliss - was a two-faced stuck-up little Madam who would get her come-uppance one day, and maybe sooner than she thinks. There wasn't a clock in the cell, but Sam guessed it to be about mid-day, the young policeman ought to be back soon he thought, and suggested to Brenda that she lock him back up now as he didn't want to get her into trouble with her husband. She was just saying how it would be alright and to stop worrying, Rory trusted her judgement, when the latch on the front door clicked and as it opened the little ting-ping of the Police doorbell sounded his return to the stationhouse. He had Lord Hurley with him.

"Brenda -" he called out round the empty police office which she was supposed to be manning. "Down here" she called back. "Down in the cellar with Sam." The two men came downstairs, all smiles.

"You're free to go Samuel," said the young policeman triumphantly. "I found Lady Felicity's purse up on the Point where she'd lost it," he continued, "exactly where you told me you had found her lying injured - she must've dropped it when she fell."

Lord Hurley piped in "I told the Constable here about our little secret, that it was I who gave you the Five Pound note as a reward for helping my daughter."

"So, I hope you'll accept my apologies and feel free to leave whenever you wish" said the young policeman swinging the cell door wide open.

"That's very kind of you Rory" said Sam, making the young bobby blush again a little with the informality "and Brenda" he turned to the young wife "next time make sure he eats a good breakfast before he goes out early in the morning again, I can hear his stomach rumbling from here" and smiled, making the young couple both laugh.

As Sam walked away from the station house towards the shops in the village Brenda looked at her husband. "See, I told you he was a decent old sort."

"Yes, but he couldn't half do with some new clothes though" said Rory solemnly as they watched the shambling six-foot-tall giant of a man making his way down the road and out of their lives, his rucksack jingling and jangling with its load of pots and pans and whatever else tied on.

"I hope we'll see him again" she said softly as they watched him go.

Chapter 4

The Reverend Jonathon Marsh

Almost the First of May. Sam's most favoured day of the year, in this, his most cherished month. The arrival of each of the four seasons was always marked by society on diaries and calendars and schedules and timetables, mainly so that people knew where they were in the journey of each passing year. To a countryman like Sam the season's happened whenever they felt like it, they each had their own special place in time where it just came together. There was a point somewhere in December or January when it felt like Winter had suddenly arrived and the weather would reach its coldest and darkest. Similarly, there was a point in March or April when Spring seemed to bounce onto the scene with all its beauty and freshness and the first daffs' were proudly standing tall. Equally as stunning there was a point in June or July when the Summer boomed out and the weather would be guaranteed to reach its brightest and warmest. And there was a point somewhere in October or November when Autumn fell upon the countryside and the days reached their most crisp and golden with the first early frosts to chill the breath.

But in May it was especially unique. A one-off point in the celestial movement of the planet across the cosmos when the passing of a year was at its peak and when everything wholesome and good happened all at once and everything came together in a harmony and clarity of purpose like no other Month in the calendar could hope to equal. Everywhere in the countryside was alive. The new lambs so tenderly cared for just a few months ago were strong and independent and frolicking happily in the fields. The sparrows and the starlings were beavering away making nests and finding mates to share them with. Ducks and swans on the rivers and lakes were beginning to divide and mark their territories, and the trees and flowers were ablaze with blossoms and blooms and buds fair to bursting. Pretty young village maids danced around the maypole hoping to attract a husband from the local farmhands and the Morris Dancers with their bells and clacking-sticks jigged about on the best pub-crawl of the year. Bliss!

Sam could spend every day of his life living in the Month of May.

Nothing died, nothing faded away, no fruits were left uneaten, no leaves were left to wither and fall. May was full of life. The Sun came up earlier every morning and went to bed later every night, the days were getting longer, and you could spend more time enjoying them. Even the stars seemed cheerier. Sleeping out amongst it all, living your life amongst it all, being free to please yourself seemed almost too much goodness for one person to have. Life couldn't really be like this all the time, not really, there had to be some darkness, some chink in the sunlight, some clouds over the horizon, Sam knew that, but for now he was happy to wake-up to the wonderful exaltation of the world in all its glory and just marvel at it all around him.

The bright early-morning sunshine had highlighted a hazy sheen of millions of tiny sparkles from the droplets of dew that seemed to cover every earthly surface for miles and miles. Including Sam. His tousled beard, not too straggly as he liked to keep it fairly well under control, was itself covered in a myriad of glittery sparkles. As were his eyebrows. He hadn't wanted to sleep out with a roof over his head, makeshift or otherwise that night as he wanted to just lay where he was - on a bed of straw out of a nearby haystack - and let the dawn wake him up all by itself. Young Brenda Page had told him that in two days' time it would be the First of May when he'd mentioned to her that often he didn't really have a clue what day it was. Except for maybe Christmas, Good Friday, Bonfire Night, those sorts of things. Days that other folk kept measure by and from observing their actions he knew for himself where he was in relation to their festivities. Other than that, he just abided by his own notions and listened to the body-clock of Life going on about him.

Except for May.

He always liked to know when it was going to be the First of May. He always began to get the feeling that it was near and would contrive to ask someone.

His breath was blowing as a puff of steam this particular May morning, just enough to remind him that the nights could still be a bit chilly and the bright morning sunshine not quite up to the full strength of high Summer, but like all the occupants of God's green and pleasant land he knew activity would bring its own reward. “Right, you old lay-about” he spoke to the invisible space three feet in front of him, “don't just lie there - let's be having you!” and he jumped up as if in answer to an unseen Sergeant-Major's command and did an impromptu calisthenics workout. “Up - down - arms stretch - knees bend - head back - up - down. That's the way you old bugger” he puffed “get that ticker going, up - down - arms stretch - knees bend - head back - up - down - start again” which he kept repeating out loud to himself all the while, exercising for a good ten minutes or more. “Whew...” he puffed to a halt, “that soon warmed you up” he said to his bit of empty space.

He stooped to put his boots on and at that instant the meadow was filled with the sound of raucous laughter, clapping, and cheering. Schoolboy clapping and cheering.

“Jolly Good...” boomed a well-spoken voice some distance behind him. As he turned to see whence the sound had come a troop of ten and eleven-year-old Boy Scouts came bounding over whooping and whistling, accompanied at the rear by their angular Scout Master. “Jonathan Marsh” he called out before him, “and this noisy lot are the 2nd Beamont Scout Troop.”

“Sam Bishop” responded Sam warmly, grinning all over his face at the sudden realisation that they must have been watching him when he'd jumped up, flailed his arms and legs all over the place, and wondered what on earth was going on. “Pleased to meet you Mr. Marsh.”

“Call me Jonathan” he invited, and as they reached each other, proffered a thin-fingered hand in friendly greeting.

“Jonathan it is,” said Sam brightly as he vigorously took hold of the Scout Master's outstretched hand in his own large care-worn palms and shook a warm friendly greeting with his new acquaintance. As the two men shook hands the troop cluttered around them both like a gaggle of geese and, like all ten and eleven-year-olds, were chattering incessantly and firing questions like an inquisitive bombardment of ack-ack guns.

‘Where do you come from Mister?' 'Did you sleep out here all night without a tent?' ' 'Ave you got a dog Mister?' And then it happened, some bright spark with a cheeky grin piped up - 'Ave you got ants in your pants?' - and that was it, they all burst out laughing.

'Ants-in-your-pants' - 'Ants-in-your-pants' they all chanted together whilst imitating Sam's spontaneous workout routine 'ee-ay-adio, ants-in-your-pants' making up an instant boy-scout singalong song and all the while jumping up and down mockingly scratching their backsides as if they really did have ants in their pants.

“That's enough boys - calm down now - you'll upset Mr Bishop.” He turned to face Sam who was by now grinning and laughing himself and clapping along in time with them. “Please accept my apologies, the little rascals don't know when to stop.” He turned back to the boys, “come on now boys, enough's enough, calm down now” although being boys, of course, they didn't.

“Roll Call...” he suddenly barked with his best Scout-Master-in-Charge voice to which all the boys instantly responded, shuffled themselves into a neat straight line, stood to attention and saluted their Commanding Officer. “Well done - well done” he said, congratulating their smartness, "stand easy." The boys relaxed but knew they were still under orders and remained silent while standing in ranks.

"Good lads really" he said to Sam, trying to bring a bit of decorum to the proceedings. "Listen boys, what say we show Mr Sam here some Beamont hospitality and invite him to camp-breakfast with us?" 'Hooray' they all shouted back in a big cheer.

"So be it - right men - FALL OUT!" and with that command they all clambered about Sam and Mr Marsh, gathered up Sam's belongings and proceeded to march him across the meadow to their camp site.

All this excitement and attention might have been a bit bewildering, but Sam took it in his stride and joined in; mind you, he didn't have much choice. The boys seemed to see him as some kind of kindred spirit, out camping in the fields just like they were, a true Boy Scout, and they all took him to their hearts. As they approached the ring of dark green bell-tents, pitched facing each other in a huge circle like an ancient iron-age settlement, Mr Marsh reminded them all that it was still very early in the morning and that before breakfast could be started there was a little matter of collecting firewood, getting the campfire going and making the camp kitchen ready. "Oh! and prayers haven't been said yet," he called out. As one they burst into action, little groups darting here and there carrying out their respective chores. Mr Marsh looked across at Sam.

"They're working for their badges, bless them" and gesturing towards his Scout Masters tent fetched a couple of folding wooden and canvas chairs for them both to sit on, like the kind that coarse fishermen use.

“Take a pew” he said “and we'll leave them to it. I've got some freshly boiled water in this kettle, we'll have a quick cup of tea for now” and the both of them sat and watched as the boys, true to their orders, got on with the business of 'making camp breakfast'. Before long everything was ready, and it was time for inspection and prayers. Sam hadn't noticed but Mr Marsh had slipped away quietly inside the tent. It was only when the Senior Scout, a pimply youth with glasses and an almost vicious looking short-back-and-sides haircut ran over to announce that Camp Breakfast was ready for inspection and Mr Marsh re-appeared at his tent-flap doorway with a “coming Stanley...” chirrup that Sam realised he'd even gone, so engrossed was he with the going's on. In that instant though, as Mr Marsh fully emerged from his canvas hideaway Sam noticed a certain difference about him. He was wearing what would colloquially be described as a dog-collar, like a shirt on the wrong-way-round. A clerical collar in fact. All of which indicated only one thing, this was a 'Man of the Cloth'. Noticing a surprised look on Sam's face as he had bent out from the flap and stood up to full height, he spoke.

“Oh - didn't I say - it's Reverend Jonathan Marsh. Part time scout leader and Vicar of the Parish of Beamont...” To say that Sam's breath had been taken away would be an understatement, but his jaw had dropped slightly, and he could feel his mouth involuntarily agape. Gathering his wits he gulped it quickly to a close, clunking his teeth together like a horse as he did so.

“Sorry Jonathan - er Reverend - er Mr Marsh, Sir, I didn't realise.”

"And why would you? - but don't be alarmed - I'm still me."

Sam smiled, "yes of course" he said.

That would explain some of Jonathan's many religious quotes earlier he thought as the two men followed young Stanley across to the camp kitchen area. "2nd Beamont Scout Troop ready for inspection Sir" said the youngster proudly, he'd obviously whipped them into shape being the oldest and Number Two to Mr Marsh in the troops' hierarchy. A grand line-up of fresh young faces, smiles beaming from ear to ear, stood to attention behind the row of trestle tables commandeered from the village hall to make-do as a servery for the food. Scout Master Marsh silently walked along the line stopping here and there occasionally to sample the breakfast food which had been prepared on the campfires blazing away in their rings of stone boulders. Two huge round frying-pans, one with bacon rashers sizzling away, the other with sausages. A big square pan filled with hot lard four inches deep into which dozens of squares of white bread had been dropped and were even now well on their way to perfect crispness. Another huge frying-pan, this one laden with eggs turning milky white with lovely golden yellow yolks and finally a large boiling-pot full to the brim with baked beans, bubbling and glooping away like an erupting volcanic mud pit. At the end of the row the three youngest members of the troop had laboriously prepared a big plateful of bread and butter. They were Cub Scouts on their first outing with the big boys and were so proud of their achievements that their little faces were lit up like beacons, all rosy cheeked and bright eyed. This is what camping was all about and the best reason so far this morning for joining the 2nd Beamont Boy Scouts Brigade! Reverend Marsh - Scout Master Marsh - congratulated the boys on a job well done.

"You'll all get your badges for this" he said exuberantly "and when we've eaten, I've got a little surprise for you all." A buzz of excitement started to get underway but was stopped in its tracks with Reverend Marsh joyfully announcing Prayers. "Lord -" he started, at which pronouncement all the boys put their hands together in prayer and bowed their heads as one. "May we thank You for this wonderful food before us - for providing us with the nourishment of our daily bread - and for the wondrous morning of this bright New Day - Amen." "Amen" they all intoned softly back to him.

"Right" he said, becoming Scout Master Marsh again, "you may serve the Camp Breakfast" at which signal the place was suddenly a hive of activity. Plates and pots, knives and forks, clatters and chinks. Disher-upper's plopping out great mounds of food onto the outstretched row of plates being held out at arm's length by their expectant recipients. Hot steaming heaps of baked beans, layers of eggs and fried bread, sizzling sausages, lovely. Soon everyone was served, including Sam and Mr Marsh, and tucking-in noisily to the feast. There was plenty to go around, enough for seconds in fact.

"There's more beans left..." said one disher-upper "and some sausages," said another.

"Any fried bread?" asked Sam with a grin, feeling conscious of the whole troop looking across at him as he'd already had four slices, "it's my favourite" he added. When breakfast was over and the camp kitchen was cleaned away Jonathan gathered the boys in a circle, sat them down on the straw bales and announced the surprise.

"Right boys, as you know our new friend Mr Bishop joined us this morning after we had all laughed at him doing his little wake-up jig" they all laughed "and while you were all getting on with the breakfast he and I had a little chat and it seems that Mr Bishop has got many hidden talents that he has learnt on his walks' over the years and I've asked him to give us a talk about some of them. He has also agreed to take us all for a hike across to Gossets Wood and teach us how to look for food and live in the wild."

Cheers and whoops of delight rose up from the gathered circle, this is what they wanted. Go off to the woods, play at being cowboys and indians, go hunting and catch their own dinner, brilliant! Mr Marsh calmed them down and introduced Sam. "Boys, say a good strong Beamont 'Hello' to Mr Samuel Bishop." Again, they cheered and whooped, and all together shouted out "HALLO MR BISHOP..." at the top of their voices.

Sam stood up and did a mock bow like a Royal Courtier then, to make them laugh, a curtsey. "Morning boys! So, you're the 2nd Beamont Scout Troop. That noisy lot I've been hearing about on my travels, 'don't go near Beamont' one farmer told me last week, them Scouts there'll knock your block off wi' all their shoutin' he reckoned." They all laughed and cheered at their fame and notoriety even though Sam was making it up.

"So, it's terrific to meet you all. My name's Samuel J. Bishop, but you can call me Sam, everybody does. I'm a Traveller, a kind of lonely wanderer. Some people call folk like me a Tramp because we tramp the roads, but I don't like that word. It makes me sound like some kind of old scrounger, some sort of scruffy good-for-nothing and yet I'm as good as the next man. I've been on the road for as long as I can remember, one way or another. You see I'm an orphan; that means that when I was younger like you, I didn't have anywhere to call home, not really. I didn't have any parents, so I had to live in an orphanage. I got moved about a bit in the beginning so didn't really get to settle down anywhere."

"Where did your parents go Mister?"

"To be honest I don't know. I was too young to remember. I think my dad died in the First World War, but I never really knew who he was, and my mum I'm not sure, I think she must have died not long after I was born because I find it hard to remember her. There was a lot of typhus going around back then. Still, never matter, that was a long time ago. My real name's not Bishop though, I was given that surname when I was about two or three. I was at a home run by a Mr Messenger, he was a big fat man with a wobbly tummy that jiggled when he laughed. He was nice." He paused for a moment in fond remembrance of a distant past.

"Anyway, whenever he got kids with no parents at all he used to give them new names: 'It'll start them off fresh in their new life...' he'd say, and his favourite way of choosing was to use games. When I was there, he was using chess. My friend was called Reginald King, another lad was called Tommy Rook. I remember a Billy Knight and then I was called Bishop. We kept our first names though; it was just our surnames that were different. Mind you, I don't know what the 'J' stands for."

He stopped as he noticed some of the boys raise their hands desperate to fire questions at him. "What was your old name?"

"I don't remember, Peters, I think."

"How long did you stay there?"

"Oh - a quite a few years."

"What did he do when he ran out of chess names?"

"Picked another game."

"What kind?"

"Oh - like - er – cards I suppose. You could be called, say, James Hart or John Diamond, that sort of thing."

"Good job he wasn't playing Snap!" quipped one cheeky youngster making them all laugh at the thought of it, which of course started them all off. "Or draughts! Or Ludo! Or Snakes and Ladders!"

"Sam Snakes and Ladders - pleased to meet you" Sam chortled.

"Or Lenny Ladders" shouted another bright spark laughing his head off at his own joke. "That's enough Leonard" interrupted Mr Marsh, patting his hands in the air so as to calm them all down "hush now."

Sam continued. "When I was old enough to look after myself, I left the home and set off to make my way in the world. There weren't many jobs around back then, work was scarce, but I was a quick learner and good with my hands. I found that the best way to get on was that if someone asked me whether I could do a particular job, I would always say 'Yes' even if I couldn't. That way I would be more than likely to be given the work, more often than not. As a result, through the years I've had a go at most things so there's not much that I can't do... Mostly I would try to get farm work, that way I would nearly always get food and lodgings thrown in. Really, that was the reason I started travelling. I liked working outdoors but always found that when one job was finished, I couldn't wait to get moving-on again. I couldn't just stick at one job for ages and ages, not like some people. I used to get bored and start daydreaming what else was there for me?" he paused, deep in thought and then brightened up, adding "I suppose there's a bit of gypsy in me..."

They'd all been listening intently and were obviously keen on hearing more but some of Sam's childhood memories had re-surfaced and he suddenly didn't feel like continuing, so to cut short his tale he quietly said "and then after a few years the war came along, and I went to Germany and then later Africa with all the other young lads. When it was over I just carried on where I had left off and here I am today, still roaming about. Living this kind of life, I suppose I've learnt lots of things about looking after myself, so you could say I'm just an overgrown boy-scout really..." he grinned at the circle of seated boys, "when you come to think of it."

Mr Marsh stood and thanked Sam by leading a quick hand-clapping response, having sensed that Sam's story had come to a somewhat quicker end than he'd expected and then turned to the troop and said, "right everyone, gather up your things and let's be away." The youngsters quickly got their kit and sorted themselves into their Pack Groups and were ready for the off. Mr Marsh walked to the front of the troop with Sam by his side, "and for today I think we'll make Mr Sam here an Honorary Scout Leader."

They all cheered. 'Hooray!' and off they went.

From the maps that Jonathan had, Sam had marked out a hike of about ten miles, across the fields where they were camped, through a small valley and into one side of Gossetts Wood. Back across the local river: the Beam; and home past the Decoy through the reed beds. He had walked in these parts before but usually on a journey through and on to somewhere else rather than actually making a point of lingering around the place, so it would make a pleasant day out for him as well. In the midday sunshine the 2nd Beamont Scout Troop looked like a gaggle of geese walking across the horizon. At their head two figures were leading the way. One stout and tall with a backpack slung over his shoulders clanking and rattling with the swaying motion of his footsteps. The other rather thin, seemingly undernourished but never-the-less as fit as a fiddle, striding out with great long gangly legs sporting a brace of lily-white knees which peeped out every now and then from under a pair of oversized khaki shorts as he walked. The owner of the legs oblivious to his comical appearance, marching ahead all nonchalant without a care in the world; except whether or not his well-built companion really could read maps because as for him, he was completely lost!

"So - are we facing North or South?" he said quietly to Sam as they came to a clearing in the trees.

"East" came the reply.

"Ah, as I thought. Boys - gather round. As Sam has decided we can stop here for a break, I thought now might be a good time for you to do a bit of map reading and try to work out where we are."

He laid out his big 'Countryside Map of English Lanes & Byways' on the grass and plonked a stone in each corner to hold it down while the boys all got their pocket compasses out. Sam sat away to one side on a large granite boulder, got out his penknife and started to peel one of the apples Jonathan had given him to carry for the boys' lunch. He silently watched the hordes wriggling about in front of him trying to work out where they were in relation to the map. Having looked like a gaggle of geese for the last half hour the assembled clump of youngsters now sounded like a gaggle of geese. Much deliberation was going on as to where they were exactly, which way they were facing and which way they had come from. Above all, which way they should go so as to continue on the right trail for the remainder of the hike. And whether they were lost or not... Scout Master Marsh came and sat alongside Sam on the boulder. As he did so his body shivered slightly; the stone was cold to his bony backside and his flimsy khaki shorts offered little protection. "So - er - we're on the right route then? - Good – Splendid -" he kept pausing trying not to look Sam straight in the eye as he spoke, "fine - Well Done."

"Right boys, anyone worked it out yet?" he said after ten more minutes or so of furious debate. Several voices announced their findings. "We're in Gossetts Woods Mr Marsh, sir," "- on the left-hand side," "- heading East." "Well done those boy's, absolutely correct, heading East: Apple anyone?" Sam could see the boggled look on Mr Marsh's face so moved over to the map, smiled, knelt down on the grass beside it and with his own compass showed everyone else how to do it.

"With your compass held steady the needle always points to North, rotate the case round so that the 'N for North' marker lines-up with it. On the side of the map is the legend, that's always got a North marker printed on it as well. Now, carefully rotate the map itself until both the 'North markers' line-up on the compass and the map. If you lay the compass down gently onto the map, still pointing correctly to North, then you know the other three ways will be correct as well. Simple. Or, you could have looked at the trees."

With that Sam smiled again, deftly re-folded the map, gave it back to Mr Marsh who popped it along with his own compass sheepishly back into one of the myriad small pockets of his anorak, called out "let's be off" stood to attention and marched off. "This way boys!" added Scout Master Marsh quickly rising up from his bum-numbing boulder and briskly trotting after Sam. When they reached the river on the opposite edge of the woods it was just going into the afternoon, so it seemed a good time to stop and make proper camp. Lunch was eaten, fish-paste sandwiches, arrowroot biscuits and orange squash.

"We'll stay for an hour or so this time so if any of you boys want to go off exploring, keep a watch on the time" said Mr Marsh making them laugh with his unintentional pun. "I see you don't wear a wristwatch yourself Sam."

"No, can't get the hang of it. I had one once. Kept forgetting to wind it up so whenever I thought to myself 'wonder what time it is?' I'd look down and the bugger'd be stopped!!" he laughed, "anyhow, I live by the land and Mother Nature's clock is good enough for me: she tells me when to wake up, when to eat, when to go to sleep, that sort of thing."

"I suppose so," he responded, "tell me, what was that about the trees?"

Sam explained that, generally speaking, you could look at tree trunks and see if they had any green moss or lichen growing up just one side. If several did and it was generally the same side on each then you could declare that to be the North facing edge. The Sun strikes the rest of the tree during the day on its voyage from east to west which keeps the opposite side permanently in the shade, damp and moist, ideal conditions for moss and the like to grow. That had to be the north side. It wasn't infallible though. If you were in a fairly dense wooded area none of the trees saw much sunshine so as a consequence damp green moss could be seen everywhere. Still, it was a fanciful thought. Sam remembered that he had promised to show the troop how to survive out in the wild without having food handed to you on a plate, as it were. There was no one out here to feed you, and if you didn't happen to have a handy packed-lunch or two on you, then you'd go hungry. Being near the river, the easiest example to show them was fishing. If it was shallow enough you could tickle a trout or two for your supper. If it was deeper, more fulsome, then a home-made fishing pole with a bent pin for a hook would do the trick, as long as you had something for bait. A bit of dried bread or some earthworms would do. Or, you could make an eel trap. Not having the time to do it properly by fashioning a basket woven from hazel twines and reed stems Sam showed them the next best thing. An old sack. Put in some smelly rotten old scroat, say a bone from the local butchers' or a dead pigeon from the woods around you and then fill the sack with straw or fern bracken. Make a cross at the top with two sticks to wedge the sack open, then lower it into the water against the flow. Stake it to the bank with rope or a sharp stick, so as not to lose it, as when it's thoroughly sodden there's quite a bit of weight there, and there you have it. One eel trap. Come back the next day and with luck several eels have slithered their way in after the smelly enticement of rotting food and due to the straw and the flow of the water, can't find their way back out again. Sam pointed out that this was fine as long as you liked eating cooked eel, as sometimes you could find yourself with twenty or thirty of the slimy little wrigglers trapped in just one night. More often than not they would all be snaggled and entwined with each other so much that if you weren't careful, you'd never be able to unravel them anyway, so the thought of eating anything so loathsome and stupid was enough to put you off outdoor living for life. Much better to remember to go shopping whenever you had the chance then you'd never be in that position in the first place. They all laughed.

Anyway, there were always wild berries to be found if you were clever and knew where to look. Along with mushrooms and ducks eggs, you very nearly had a cooked breakfast in the making. If you were really keen the odd spit-roasted wood pigeon or mallard went down a treat; if you were an uncaring carnivorous megalomaniac hunter of dinner-on-the-wing and didn't mind all that killing and gutting stuff that went with it. Most of the boys got the message. Sam's life wasn't all wonderful. Tramping around the countryside year in year out wasn't a bed of roses, sometimes it was no bed at all, and you slept where you were out of sheer exhaustion and weariness. And when it rained, well... Mr Marsh realised that Sam had intentionally decided to bring the troop back to earth with a bump as they'd all eagerly announced on arrival at the river as to what fun it would be to hunt their own dinner or catch their own supper: little knowing what it really entailed, and he was pleased Sam had not painted too rosy a picture of it.

"Let's have a singsong" he said, trying to break the moment "and then we'll start to make our way back to camp."

"What about the Decoy reed beds Sir?" called out one young voice with a smirk and a memory too sharp for his own good.

"Another time Clifford - another time." And that was that.

Actually, it was a good thing they'd set off when they had, as Sam pointed to a quickly darkening sky, "too early for nightfall, must be a storm coming in," he said quietly to Mr Marsh as they led a singing crocodile of boy scouts swiftly back to camp and the relative safety of their canvas tents. "You never did tell me what you were doing this morning" said Mr Marsh to Sam as they crossed the field where the circle of bell-tents awaited their tired occupants.

"Just waking up. At my age I'm a bit stiff some mornings so I have a quick jig. Apart from that I woke up early to see the dawn come up, as it's the First of May today, my favourite day." "Oh, I see..." Mr Marsh didn't say anymore.

The pack leaders set their charges about the business of the moment, getting supper ready and boiling a big vat of cocoa for bedtime. The storm held off and so as darkness fell Sam sang them one of his folksongs he'd picked up on his travels. Or had he remembered it from school? he couldn't recall, 'The Ballad of Barbara Allen' - it was his special favourite. In the distance a train whistle hooted a soulful phwoo-woo and the sound of its wheels on the tracks carried across the still, damp, fog-laden night air - jiggedy-jig jiggedy-jig jiggedy-jig - sending the last of the dozing worn out campers off to their tents to sleep. Maybe some to dream; maybe some to smile, and maybe some to cry; maybe to snuggle and maybe to whimper. After all, they weren't all tough weather-worn old codgers like Sam who was out like a light the minute his head hit the pillow despite the thunder and lightning in the early hours.

"Goodnight Sam" said the Reverend Jonathan Marsh, "and God Bless..."

The next morning everyone was in a quieter more sombre mood. The day was dull and overcast. Without the sun to cheer them everyone just went about their chores matter-of-factly. It was also packing-up day, which didn't help. They'd only had two nights under canvas but had got the taste for it. Scout Master Marsh promised them that next time he would try and make it a week. Reverend Marsh reminded them that it was only due to the kindness of their Mum's and Dad's for letting them go in the first place and of the people in the village who helped to make it all possible so they should be thankful for the time they did have. The verger for rallying around the district to borrow all the tents and camping gear. Farmer Knowles for transporting them all out here with his flat-bed trailer and the village grocer for supplying the food. They should remember that when bob-a-job week came around and maybe give a six-pennorth' extra for free, by way of a thank-you. They all nodded their agreeance. No hips' and hoorays' this time though, just quiet acknowledgement. On the dot, eleven o'clock, and Farmer Knowles' tractor pulled into the field. The troop loaded their gear. Sam gathered his things and made to leave, as he turned to wave goodbye Mr Marsh slipped off the back of the trailer and walked over to him, "come with us Sam - I'd like you to come and see my Church and our village – and the boys would love to have you with us," he paused, "and I'd be honoured to put you up for a few days, if that's alright with you".

"Very kind of you Jonathan, but I've got to push on, places to go, people to see, things to do" he bumbled unconvincingly.

"Sam - please come, I've got a job for you, something I need some help with", his face looked quite genuine, and his words were spoken with a plaintiff sincerity which Sam couldn't easily ignore.

"So be it Reverend - so be it" and with that the two men hitched themselves up on to the back of the trailer and away it went.

Sam noticed Mr Marsh looking back wistfully at the place where they had been camped, his eyes all blank and staring as if deep in thought, somewhere else. They didn't talk much after that. The boys sang a couple of choruses of 'Ten Green Bottles'. No one was really relishing going home after such high adventure: the day was still dull and overcast, where was the Sun when you needed it? An hour later all the boys had been safely deposited with their respective parents and Sam was following Mr Marsh through the small village churchyard toward the vicarage. It was a large house to one side of the small parish church, somewhat overpowering it: built at a time when the local vicar might have had aspirations of greatness, his position in the community being of a high-standing nature and mixing with the gentry on every possible occasion. Turning a blind eye when the local Squire got the odd village girl pregnant but chiding the menfolk for poaching on his Lordship's land in the same breath. Never mind their hungry children, Oh no! God would provide, as long as they weren't all wicked sinners - then woe-betide you for stealing. These days though it was just a great red brick monstrosity plonked by the side of the pretty little Portland stone church, and completely out of character. A nightmare to heat and absolutely useless for one man to have to live in all alone. In fact, Jonathan Marsh had found it easier just to live downstairs, converting the rarely used drawing-room into a bedroom-cum-study and the breakfast room into the parish office. Not for him the trappings of the high-and-mighty, no array of servants and cooks and so on to entertain passing dignitaries should they stop by, just a humble part-time housekeeper to help here and there running the place.

It would soon be 1960 and the world had changed. The last decade had seen a noticeable speeding-up of life since the dark despairing days of the war and the position of a parish vicar in the scale of things was not that far removed from the local Bobby' the Doctor or the District Nurse. Come to think of it, even the village Postman and pub Landlord were on a par with the vicar. Noted citizens of the Parish, usually on the Parish Council, people who the local's trusted and could look up to. Mind you, out of all of them the parish priest was usually the most revered. He saw the inhabitants of his village, his flock as it were, through all their trials and tribulations. At Christenings to welcome the new-born into the world. At Confirmations to welcome the young into the fold. At Weddings to join together the happy couples' and finally at Funerals to pass the dearly departed into the next Kingdom. The whole Circle of Life passed before him. He felt privileged to be part of it, and for Jonathan it was his whole reason for being. He only needed one thing to make his life complete, a wife and a family.

"Right Sam, you can have the spare room - second left along the hallway." Pointing down the passageway from the front door Mr Marsh gestured to Sam to walk on, "I don't bother to use the upstairs, no point, only me in the place." They were standing in the large entrance lobby of the vicarage. It was a grand wood-panelled affair with a high ceiling opening to the full height of the upstairs landing. All the downstairs rooms seemed to lead off the main hallway. Sam walked ahead as Mr Marsh had suggested and opened the door into an agreeable bright and airy downstairs bedroom: obviously a former dining room by the looks of the serving hatch in one wall and a large tile fronted fireplace in another. A fireplace that was aglow with the welcoming flames of a roaring coal fire. Jonathan popped his head around the door-jar as Sam walked in.

"Ah good - Mrs Hopkins has been in - she's my housekeeper you know - hopefully she's managed to get all the fires going - this old house can be deathly cold even in the summer."

Sam though it was roasting, but then there was a bit more of him than the nine-stone stick-insect that was Mr Marsh, so he supposed it was alright. Have to open the windows at night though, it would get stifling in here later, especially to an outdoors man like Sam. He laid out his meagre belongings, combed his hair and then went in search of Mr Marsh. From the clanking sound of a coke-fired boiler being stoked Sam deduced that he was to be found in the kitchen and as that was invariably at the back of a house, he made his way along the hallway and through one of the adjacent doors.

"Nope, that looks like an office - bit like that young copper's house a while back" he mumbled. He tried another. "Downstairs lavvy' - handy to know in case I wakes up in the middle of the night" he mumbled again, and then finally at the far end of the hall, success, "afternoon Vicar!"

"Oh, hallo Sam, come in. Mrs Hopkins got the stove going for me but it's a bit temperamental. I'm just trying to get a kettle going for a cup of tea."

"Let's have a go - I used to be pretty good at these in the army. My 'oppo Nobby Clarke reckoned I could make a cup of tea anywhere. Storm the Reichtesgaden, easy, but make a pot of tea, ask old Sammy he'd say."

"Do you still keep in touch?"

"He was killed in North Africa..."

"Oh, I am sorry."

"Ne'er mind - long time ago, nigh on fifteen years... shame really, I'd just put the kettle on too," and he smiled a wry smile.

Jonathan was too young to have fought in the war so he couldn't really equate with Sam's jaunty remark to his friend's sad ending, but he had met many old soldiers in his theological career, and they all exhibited the same light-hearted bravado. He supposed it was the only way they could get through it. The next stray bullet could be for them. What could you do but see the funny side of things and to try and carry on. Look at Sam, no one in the world to worry about him or care how he is doing, but does he let it bother him, no, he just keeps on travelling the country, bumping into folk, helping where he can and just enjoying being alive. Not much to ask for.

"What say we have this cup of tea and then I take you on a grand tour of my little church and the village and then after we can call in to The Swan for a bite to eat."

Sam liked the sound of that as he always felt pub food was the best, a lovely hot pie and a pint would go down a treat a little later, but there was snag.

"I haven't really got the spare money Jonathan - I'm trying to keep a little by for emergencies." "Not to worry Sam, as I said, I've got some work for you so let's call it a sub' and we'll hear no more of it."

That evening they spent a happy few hours in the company of the local villagers at The Swan Inn. Most of the dads had heard the story of 'ants-in-your-pants Sam' from their excited young off-spring and insisted on hearing the tale again, from the horses-mouth as it were. Sam was only too happy to oblige. Although being a loner wandering from place to place without any real roots, he always found the folk in a village pub to be the friendliest collection of people he could ever hope to come across. He was the sort of person who could make friends with anybody and everybody, seemingly all at once, within minutes of meeting them. A pub full of people and every one of them a friend of 'Old Sam'. It wasn't long before he was up in front of them re-enacting his morning exercises although now, after a couple of pints of jack-cider it looked more like a squawking chicken about to lay an egg... Someone asked what he was doing out there in the first place to which Sam explained about his personal beliefs surrounding the First of May. How it meant for him a kind of renewal, a spiritual awakening of Nature more glorious than the first day of Spring. About how he made it a point of knowing exactly where he was every May Day by keeping notes in his journal and always gave special mention to it. Then he belched a deep belly-wobbling burp of cidery gas and made everyone laugh; it was his way of not letting the evening get too solemn.

Jonathan had sat listening intently, especially at the mention of a journal. Inside he was brimming with happiness. If only Sam but knew, that he most probably held the key to all of Jonathan's anxieties and worries: then he might not have been so ready to accept all the free drinks that were being offered him and, in the morning, he wouldn't have a thumping headache to contend with. But that was the morning, tonight was now, and everyone was having a good time; even Jonathan who tried to join-in some of the songs Sam was singing, but as they were of the bawdier variety gathered through years of visiting pubs up and down the length and breadth of the country, he didn't really have a chance. Mostly he didn't even know the words. Some young lad said 'let's sing some Lonnie Donnegan' to which Sam boomed back.

"Donnie Lonn - a - Gone - Again! Who's he???" and made the whole assembly roar with his mispronunciation...

Despite the quantity of ale supped Sam awoke the next morning just as he always did, bright and early and gasping for a cup of tea. He figured that Jonathan wouldn't mind if he popped into the kitchen quietly and helped himself. In return he made a point of getting the stove going, filling the scuttle with fresh coke-nuts and getting a tank-full of water heated-up for washing and so on. When it was a more decent hour he would take Jonathan a cup of tea. Six o'clock should do it...

"Sam - Good morning to you," said Jonathan as Sam opened the door and walked into the bedroom, "what time is it?" As always Sam instinctively looked down at his wrist to the space where a watch would have normally been visible, "just gone six" he said, quite knowingly, despite there being nothing on his forearm to actually look at, "made you a cup of tea."

"Thank you, most welcome."

"I'm gonna have me a nice hot bath, if that's alright by you?"

"Fine."

"Only I've had the boiler stoked for over an hour now so should be good and hot, and I don't get much chance of that out on the road."

"Be my guest" said Mr Marsh, wondering how on earth Sam could be up so early all bright and cheerful after the night they'd had last night in the pub, "must have the constitution of an ox...".

After a light breakfast Jonathan walked Sam over to the Church Hall to show him the work he had been referring to. It was a bit run down and in need of a good lick of paint; the trouble was it was put-up before the war and had been used by all the community in that time for all manner of things, without anyone really taking care of it and now looked a bit worse-for wear.

"The Scout Troop meet here every Thursday - that's how I got involved" he said as they surveyed the sorry looking building, "and the W.I. hold jumble sales most weeks. We've got the paint together but could never really afford to pay anyone to put it on for us - I wondered if you might volunteer, in return for free board and lodgings at the vicarage. What do you think?"

"Well, it's a bit of a state but we'll give it a go."

"Splendid - splendid," he replied with a warm smile "I knew you'd say yes, right, where do we start?"

"First things first, let's get the kettle on. Kitchen through here?" and he gave Mr Marsh a slap on the back to fair knock the wind out of him and they both laughed.

"You and your tea" chuckled the Reverend Marsh.

Before long they had made a good start on the decorating, Sam had washed over all the old paintwork with sugar-soap while Mr Marsh had gone around with the dustsheets; covering the piano and stacking the tables and chairs into the middle of the hall so that they could work around them more easily. Sam had knocked up a sign and pinned it to the Church Hall door.

"Closed for Re-decoration - Men at Work" it read.

Slowly the day wore-on and the two of them gained a kind of silent rapport. Each one doing his own part and yet, as if unsaid, both knowing the others mind as to what should be done next. In Sam's case it was easy, he had painted and decorated many times before, so it was second nature. Not so for Jonathan, he had never had much call for doing this kind of thing; still, he was a hardworking and cheery companion. Occasionally he could be heard softly whistling a tune, a hymn maybe, as they worked. Sam, as always, quietly hummed his favourite song,

Barbara Allen, when he was in a quiet mood. As they walked home across the churchyard that evening Jonathan seemed far-away again. It had been a mild early-summer's day and was now a warm summer's evening. The last rays of the Sun caught the wispy cloud edges hanging in the sky, like giant ostrich feathers, as it dipped majestically and serenely below the horizon causing that lovely red glow to emanate across the blueness like a heavenly shroud.

"Red Sky at Night - Shepherd's Delight" said Sam soulfully as he stood for a few minutes to take it all in. Jonathan too stopped.

"Isn't it glorious," he said after a moments pause, "you could just drink it in."

"My sentiments entirely Jon, and all the better for sharing it with someone who appreciates the sweet grandeur of it all."

"Yes, Sam. God was truly at His most wondrous when He made the sunrises' and the sunsets' over this beautiful Earth of ours and it would indeed be a dream to spend one's life in the company of another; to always be able to witness it together," he looked all dreamy and distant again.

They stood for a few more moments and then turned to cross behind the chancel and into the backdoor of the vicarage. Sam followed; a little perplexed this time with Jonathan's starry-eyed far-away demeanour, and he resolved to find out what lay at the heart of this kindly soul, who was obviously longing for something that he didn't seem to be able to achieve. After dinner tonight he decided, they would sit quietly reading and he could bring the subject up, surreptitiously at first, then hopefully more openly. The good vicar of Beamont was too young a man to be living his life on an unreachable dream, he deserved fulfilment as much as the next man. There had to be a way of helping.

Mrs Hopkins had left a beef stew bubbling away on the range, complete with suet dumplings, and had laid out the table for the pair of them complete with a bottle of brown ale each and a note to the vicar that 'she'd be in, in the morning and they should leave the dishes seeing as how they'd both been working so hard at the paintin' all day today. Oh - and the locum priest says are you enjoying your 'oliday's? Yours truly, Gladys. PS: Mrs Hopkins.'

Never one to shirk his duties Sam duly took no notice of the letter and did all the washing-up anyway. "Can't abide to see a place untidy" he said to Jonathan, who in turn tidied-up the dinner things and cleared away the table. Now would be a good time thought Sam, if I can get him talking while we work. "Tell me about life in this Parish then Jonathan. What's it like being the Vicar here?"

That was a question which would need such a long reply that Sam was sure to find the answer to Jonathan's dreaminess hidden in it somewhere. He needn't have worried. The young man standing next to him wanted desperately to tell him something about himself, in the hope that Sam might provide the answers he was looking for.

"Well, I first came here when I was at theological college in Shepton. They needed a new priest, and I was put forward as a possible replacement, ready for when I qualified. I was immediately taken with the place and couldn't believe my luck when at twenty-five the diocese sent me here to take-up the reins. That was eight years ago, and I've loved every minute of it."

"Have you never thought to get married, start a family here?" This was the very chance Mr Marsh had been waiting for; the very question he wanted Sam to ask.

"Well, actually Sam, I wanted to ask you something first, and depending on your answer, I might then be able to answer the question for you." They quickly finished the washing-up and left the teacloths hanging over the range to dry. "Let's go into the front-room and we can talk some more, bring those other two bottles of beer and I'll tell you a tale."

It seemed that Mr Marsh had in fact met a young woman from a nearby village not long after he had arrived in Beamont. She was only seventeen at the time and was having a difficult time looking after her elderly parents. They were both virtually bedridden, so the young girl found it quite exhausting coping on her own. Folk did their best to help, including the Church, and that's how Jonathan had come across her. As those early years in Beamont went by, the two of them got to know each other more deeply, but a romance was out of the question; she could never leave her parents for too long as they needed her constant attention. Then one summer, a few years ago, a traveller wandered into the village and took an instant liking to the young woman and her parents: so much so that she was able to spend a few special weeks with her young man, who by now she had grown quite fond of. The kindly old visitor stayed and took care of her mother and father. Nothing seemed too much trouble for him, he took it all in his stride. Sam moved to the fire and self-consciously started to rake amongst the coals with a brass poker as Mr Marsh continued his story.

She hadn't had a break in years. The young couple dreamed of the day they could be together properly, married and in a home of their own. They went out on picnics together. She taught him to ride, they enjoyed each other's company making every moment last. As for the stranger he excelled himself, arranging for a couple of wheelchairs to be borrowed from the Red Cross and taking the parents out to the beach for a day-out. His well-built body and large powerful arms more than easily coped with lifting them out of bed and into their chairs. It was a day they would always treasure.

Mr Marsh opened the second bottle of brown ale and refilled Sam's glass. He noticed Sam staring into the flames of the fire, almost hypnotically. He filled his own glass and sat back down again in the old leather armchair and continued the tale. The young woman felt renewed and invigorated. She had been set free. Her spirit had been lifted and the burden of her responsibilities taken away. She knew it couldn't last, so did he, but they tried not to think about it; for now, they just wanted to have a little bit of happiness for themselves. Six years had gone by since then and the young couple were still apart. They tried to spend time with each other, but it was difficult, they were resolved to make the best of it.

Mr Marsh stopped.

Sam had sat back down on the sofa and was slowly twirling his empty beer glass in the palm of his hands.

He didn't speak.

Nor for that matter did Mr Marsh. He sat silently, sipping the last few mouthfuls of his beer, stood up after a while and raked the fire down to cool the ashes for the morning. They didn't say anything to each other for a full half hour, both just sitting, staring, watching the coals changing from red to grey as they slowly lost their heat to the big draughty room. After a while Jonathan spoke.

"It was you, wasn't it? You were the visitor who helped Jenny and I, you're the one..."

Sam looked up, his curly beard all but hiding a soft smile. "No - not me, I don't reckon I've been in these parts' before, must've been someone else," he tried to make it sound as convincing as he could, "must be mistaken."

"I wasn't sure at first. I mean, the chances of you actually being the same person travelling these byways; and me coming across you like that in the middle of a field on a damp May morning, seem too remote to be true. But there you were, and here you are." He walked towards the kitchen doorway ready to make his usual night-time cup of cocoa, "yet as soon as you started talking about yourself, your affinity with the First of May, your journal, I knew it was true." He turned through the open door and began to fill the saucepan with enough milk for two cups.

Sam followed behind and stood looking into the kitchen, his body framed by the doorway. "And you want me to help again..."

Jonathan, who had his back to Sam, smiled, a kind of relieved smile of extreme happiness. He was half afraid that his guesswork would have proven to be wrong, but he didn't dare admit it, not even to himself. Sam was definitely the one and there was no mistake. He finished stirring the now boiling milk and poured out two large mugs. Placing them on a tray with a small plate of digestives he beckoned Sam back into the front-room which by now was quite cold. Perhaps he shouldn't have raked the fire down so soon he thought, because now that Sam had confirmed his suspicions, he didn't really feel he could just leave it at that. He would have to know more. He wanted to know everything.

"What I don't understand is why you disappeared like you did. The very day that Jenny was bringing me over to meet you. She was very upset that you'd gone without saying goodbye."

Sam looked across at him solemnly. "I don't like to get too involved. Once folk start taking to me too much I moves on. Young Jennifer, she was a lovely lass, I just felt sorry for her and when she said her and her young man didn't get any time together, well, it seemed like the right thing to do."

"All she could remember of you was your strange tale about the Month of May, I don't even recall her mentioning your name?"

"No, probably not."

"But she's never forgotten what you did for us, and she often reminisces about that time we had together."

"Well, I'm pleased to hear it, Jonathan my young friend, that's as it should be, remember yourselves, not some old duffer like me." They both smiled at each other.

"Her mother died in the September that year, which was hard for Jenny, but it was a Blessed release." Sam expressed his sorrow and inquired as to Jennifer's father.

"Not too good I'm afraid," Jonathan paused a moment, "maybe you'd like to go over and visit them in the morning?"

"What about the painting?"

"I'm afraid that was just a ruse, a couple of the dads have already volunteered for that; I so wanted to get to know you better, I had to find out if you were the one. Jenny's father hasn't long to go and has sometimes talked of you, the visitor who took him on a picnic. It would be a wonderful gesture if you could go over, before it's too late..."

"So be it Jon, we'll go over first thing tomorrow."

"God Bless you Sam," and they shook hands.

As Sam finished up in the bathroom and made ready for bed, Jonathan Marsh mumbled softly to his reflection in the mirror "God does indeed work in mysterious ways his wonders to perform, and Jenny my love, tomorrow you'll be as awed as I am with Mr Samuel J Bishop." He called out a 'good night' parting to Sam, said a prayer of thanks and then went to bed himself.

A few days later Jennifer's father died. He'd had one more day outside with his oft remembered friend, they'd reminisced and chatted about the war, the summer's before it all started, drunk hot tea from a flask and sat listening to the robins and blackbirds trilling their far away lament as the sun had slowly set.

Sam wouldn't pass this way again for probably another four or five years, or maybe more. The way he walked and wandered about, it might even take him longer, but he knew one day he'd be back. As he 'gave away this woman' he whispered quietly to the young bride, “he'll take good care of you lass - so you enjoy yourself d'ye hear,” and gave her a hug.

Chapter 5

Barbara Henderson, the Devon beauty

"Thanks for the lift..."
"You'm welcome Sammy," called back the driver, "an I 'ope's you gets them trousers." Sam smiled and waved as the van pulled off with its cheery occupant whistling-away to some tune or other. He wasn't sure what it was but at least it was melodic which was fine. And anyway, he'd carried Sam a good fifteen miles since breakfast, so it didn't matter that he'd whistled the whole time the same unknown tune; he'd even contrived to drop him off a stone's throw from where he wanted to be. Well, a few miles walk but that didn't bother Sam. He never expected to be this far down the coast so early in the season so he couldn't have asked for more. It was mid-June now and Summer was decidedly on the way. The days were warmer and the night's so long that you could almost see to read a book still at ten o'clock in the evening. The longest day in the great cosmic movement of the Earth was definitely getting closer, he could feel it.

Along the road, he'd seen signs announcing the "County Show" and had told his van driving companion of his desire to find a new pair of trousers for the Summer - well, 'second-hand' new - and how the County Shows and Gypsy Fairs were the best place to look for bargains. He'd saved four pounds eleven shillings in his rainy-day tin and would treat himself, maybe a new hat wouldn't go amiss... Following a steady trail of traffic and foot-walkers it wasn't long before Sam was rummaging about the stalls and searching out his quarry. If he could find a decent looking pair of trousers today, then this evening he could stroll into The Cavendish Arms looking quite smart, reacquaint himself to the Landlady quite proudly, and sweep her off her feet all over again. That's if she remembered him that is.

Mapleton was a thriving sea-side town just inside the borders of Devon from the west side of Dorset. The river that separated the two counties was a natural marker for the county line and flowed as it had always done, straight to the bay and the open sea. He didn't always go this way on his trek to the West Country but every time Sam had come by these ways the place seemed to be getting bigger. More houses were being built, extra roads, a new school and a cottage-hospital. What with two cinemas and a dozen or so pubs the place seemed to be positively agog with activity. It was too much for Sam really, he liked the quiet backwaters. The country lanes and open spaces, the Low Road as he called it. Farmers' fields and hayricks, not guesthouses and penny-arcades, neon signs and 'teddy boys'. Sam had written these thoughts and comments in his journal the last time he was here, he remembered thinking how it might be the next time he saw it. Would it be even bigger, brasher maybe. Hopefully not.

As he walked over the town bridge and into the square beyond, he was glad that his prophecy hadn't come true, it was still quite pleasant. He had also written how well he'd gotten-on with Mrs Henderson - Barbara - the Landlady at the Cavendish, and how she'd remembered him from his previous visits to

Mapleton. Apparently, his knack of spontaneously bringing her pub to life with his singsongs and taletelling was something else she'd always remembered. He was rather hoping she would still remember. He was hoping she'd still want to cook him breakfast-in-bed, that she'd still find him 'strong and caring - gentle and kind' to remind her of the nights' they spent together after closing time. He was hoping.

That evening, resplendent in a new pair of dark-brown corduroys and a smart new hat, he made his way across the town centre and into the public bar of The Cavendish Arms. The Licensee Notice above the door still bore the name 'Mrs B Henderson' on it so Sam knew she was still running the place, but would she remember him? Would he have changed much in the last few years - would she? Sure, he was a little older, but underneath the gruff exterior there was still a little twinkle when he smiled and winked his eye. A roguish charm that, had he been a more settled kind of person instead of a gentleman-of-the-road, could easily have swept many a woman's feet off the ground and make her heart miss a beat. After all, in his way he was quite handsome. A full head of hair, light brown in colour, with bright sparkling eyes and a rugged care-worn face that never failed to greet you with a big wide grin and a laughing smile to match... His strong back and shoulders and broad powerful chest made for great physical strength in work yet his hands when handling sick or injured animals could be as gentle as a child's. There was power in his whole being yet never was there any malice. Even when being sworn at and cursed by unknowing passers-by who only saw a 'filthy old tramp' and a 'scrounger'. He never let other peoples' judgements make him angry. They didn't know the real 'him' so it didn't matter. Mrs Henderson knew and wasn't afraid to show it.

In fact, with his new clothes, sun-tanned rugged face, huge overcoat and haversack, he could have been taken for an Explorer just back from the Himalayas or somewhere, with tales of derring-do: a dead ringer for Sir Edmund Hillary or Walter Scott or someone, who could say? But even so, he was a bit anxious the very moment he walked through the pub doors and into the bar, for all that.

The pub was about half full, a young barmaid served him a pint of brown and mild, some people were playing cards in a corner, a darts match was in progress. A singer was taking a break from his performing; his guitar leaning against a wall, and Mrs Henderson was at the other end of the bar holding court with a group of ladies from the Licensed Victuallers Association. At least that's what they looked like to Sam, all floral cretonne frocks, hats and handbags; with make-up thick faces and strings of fake pearls around their fat necks. They could hardly be a deputation from the W.I. Only old married landladies cum ex-brassy barmaids could have turned into that little lot. Rather than interrupt the gathering, Sam quietly moved to a side table and savoured his first pint for a week or so. The guitar playing folk singer came back and with a quick re-tune of his strings began his second set of the evening. A steaming plate of sausage and mash with brown onion gravy was soon served at Sam's table.

"Do you fancy anything with it?" said the young barmaid suggestively, causing Sam to gulp unexpectedly on his beer, "Er - no - um - thanks, my dear."

"No mustard nor nothing?"

"Er, no, it's fine like it is, honestly."

"Okay my lover, just as you likes," and with that she turned and wiggled her way through the tables and back to the bar. Incredulous disbelief must have been etched onto Sam's face for a minute or so as he found himself staring dazedly across the pub after her, wondering if he had really just been propositioned by a slip of a girl young enough to be his daughter, or had he imagined it? But it must have been true, there in front of him was the dinner he'd ordered for himself not fifteen minutes earlier. Ah well.

As the evening wore on Sam quietly sat in the corner supping his way through another couple of pints, listening contentedly to the musician playing and singing his heart out; clapping appreciatively at the end of every song and occasionally sneaking a glance over to where Mrs Henderson and her pals were gathered, to see if they'd finished yet. He didn't want to just go over and say hello straight out, he hadn't seen her for the best part of three years and to say he was still anxious about it, well that was an understatement.

She was probably the only woman in Sam's life that he'd actually felt something for in a romantic sense and whom he'd shared a bed with. He couldn't just go over there and say 'Hello' like it was no big deal, he'd have to bide his time and pick the right moment; although with the clock ticking away and the evening fast coming to a close he'd have to think of something soon or miss her completely. As luck would have it the singer announced that he only had time for a few more songs and did anyone have any special requests, so Sam took his chance and leaned over to speak to him.

"Do you know '*The Ballad of Barbara Allen*'? It's an old English folk song" he whispered.

The singer looked a little perturbed, "I know the tune, but I can't say as I know all of the words...." Sam frowned slightly, then his face lit up, he'd had an idea.

"Ladies and Gentlemen" started the singer, "we've had our first request, and it's for a traditional folk song to which I'll play the accompaniment, and my good friend here will sing the words." Not everyone in the pub took any notice, in particular the youngsters with their slick-backed hair and drain-pipe trousers, but plenty of the older customers stopped their yacketing in order to sit and listen. Being a big man, Sam's huge chest and lung capacity made for a good strong powerful voice, not as deep as a bass, more mellow and flowing like a baritone but he always sang this one softly and his kindness and passion shone through the performance.

"*...In London Town where I was born – there was a fair maid dwellin'...*" as he started the hubbub died to a soft hush. "... *Her name was Barbara Allen...*". He'd barely finished the first verse when standing right in front of him was Mrs Henderson with a warm smile and a gleam on her face, wagging her finger at him and silently mouthing the words "what are you doing here?" He smiled back, pleased with himself that he'd finally worked out a way of attracting her attention and then carried on with the song. It was clear she hadn't forgotten him. Their eyes never wavered from each other's gaze. In fact, he could see a soft glistening sheen of tears welling up as he carried on singing; it was either the song, or her pleasure in seeing him again. It didn't matter either way to Sam, he was singing it for her tonight as he had often done many times before in this very pub. It was their song. It didn't matter about the sadness in the words. If love could be given a shape or a form, an image or an energy, then the space between them would be sparkling with millions of tiny little flashes of electric-blue light, dancing about every which way, colliding with each other and bouncing back again.

By now the throng of customers had all but stopped what they were doing and were silently watching and listening. There was their landlady, stood in front of a grizzled old giant of a man, looking every inch a woman in love - all starry eyed - being serenaded for all intents and purposes by what looked like her long-lost sweetheart as if just back from the War's. Smiles of recognition began to break out on the faces of some of the older onlookers, Sam Bishop was back. There'd be some fun tonight.

When he finally finished the song there was a loud cheer and an exuberant round of applause rang out. Sam stood up and did a dainty bow to his audience, just to make everyone laugh, then turned to Mrs Henderson.

"Hello old girl," he said with a smile.

"Here - less of the old! you cheeky so-and-so," she giggled back and gave him a hug then planted a big kiss straight full on his lips. Her warm soft mouth caressed him so delicately and lovingly and her fragrance sparked instant memories of being close together. He should have married Mrs Henderson. What a fool. Still, never mind, it was lovely to be back, standing here in her arms again, holding her tight and feeling her body squeezing up to his. He could have let that kiss last forever. "Put 'im down!" "'Ere, you'm better stop to breathe in a minute!" "Looks like she's eatin' 'im..."

A slightly red-faced landlady, realising that everyone was watching, coughed nervously and made as if to straighten her hair and re-adjust her dress like women do, then she laughed. How daft it must have looked, a woman of her age getting all embarrassed and steamy-eyed.

"Rusty -" she called out to the red-haired barmaid who had served Sam earlier, "a malt whisky for my best friend Mr Samuel J Bishop, and I'll have a gin an' it' - second thoughts, make them doubles." "Right-on Babs" she called back, all mod-speak like.

As they both walked to the bar people who knew Sam from old strode over and patted him on the back and shook his hands. "Nice to see you Sam old lad" said one well-wisher. "Good to have you back," said another. "You couldn't 'ave come at a better time" said someone else.

All the while Sam and Barbara holding hands, and her leading him to the bar like a puppy on a lead. He didn't mind though. He'd told her once before that it was a woman like her that he'd fought for in the war, that he'd been prepared to die for. He didn't know it would be her at the time though, he just knew it would be for someone exactly like her; he knew he would meet her one day, all he'd have to do was wait. Mind you, it was a daft way of declaring your love for some future somebody, storming a machine-gun post in broad day-light so that you could rescue your best mate lying wounded in the mud. "I'll go out and fetch him Sir, just hold this rifle for me a minute."

"Do you have anyone back home Private?"

"No, but if I don't make it, give my photo to some good-looking lady when you get back to Blighty, tell her I'd have loved to have met her. Here Jack - lend us your tommy-gun..." and with that he was off. Of course, he did get back and it was then that he realised that Fate was lending a hand. He wasn't destined never to meet up with someone, to live his adult life like his childhood years, completely alone. He just didn't know how long it was going to take before he would find her, so he was more than happy to wait. That her name was Barbara was a double bonus. As a young boy in the orphanage, he'd always liked singing, and when the choir were asked to do *Barbara Allen* for the first time he was enthralled. There was just something about it. Sometimes he'd be quietly walking across the fields and moors and be gently humming it to himself. It seemed to remind him of days gone by. Where he'd come from, where he was going to, and what he'd achieved along the way; he couldn't explain it, it just did.

An hour later the last customer had gone, and Mrs Henderson had locked up for the night, at last she and Sam were alone. "You will stay tonight?" she asked him all coyly, not wishing to force him into anything, "that's if you've nowhere else to go..."

"How about a lovely hot bath?" he said. She smiled at Sam's suggestion.

"Give me a minute an' I'll go an' run the water, come upstairs and make yourself at home." Fifteen minutes later they were both laying together in a steaming hot bubble bath, foamy perfume wafting through the rooms with all the steamy vapour floating about and misting-up the mirrors. Sam had brought up two bottles of sweet cider from the pub and they were both drinking and laughing. Mrs Henderson was lovely. She had no qualms or hang-ups with Sam. She had undressed in the bedroom, put on a silky nylon dressing-gown and strolled all naked and see-through to the bathroom where Sam was waiting for her. It was like old times. He should have married her when he'd had the chance but there you go.

It was about eight years ago, fifty' or fifty-one', he couldn't be sure, when he had first come this way through this particular town, although it was a lot smaller then, it seemed, and he happened across the pub. Barbara and her husband Frederick were the Licensees. Fred had been shelled' in the war and wasn't really *au-fait* with the world around him. He'd lost a leg and was slowly going blind and deaf, and to cap it all he was developing leukaemia. The day-to-day running of the pub had fallen on Barbara's shoulders ever since and that year Sam had strolled into the bar innocently searching for a hot meal and a pint to wash it down with. Being an old soldier himself, he couldn't just pass through like on his normal travels, so he decided to stay awhile and help out. It was a difficult time. He stayed three months in all. He never got to Cornwall that year, but it was worth the sacrifice.

When he did finally move on Barbara had got herself together and was running things a lot better. She'd had the license changed over to her name and employed some part-time barmaids and the brewery had helped by putting in a lad to do all the heavy lifting. Shift the barrels, heave the crates, that sort of thing, the jobs that Sam had been doing. She was sad to see him go when the time came as they'd grown fond of each other's company. They had the same wicked sense of humour, she'd call him an old bugger, he'd call her big bristols, she'd counter with all-mouth-an-no-trousers, and all the while they'd be serving customers who thought it was a hoot. Especially when Sam would give an impromptu concert from behind the bar of some of his songs.

Fred wasn't getting any better and really, he probably never would. She made him as comfortable as she could. They'd been through some ripe old times together one way and another, had two kids along the way, a boy and a girl, and had done alright for themselves with the pub. If only the bloody war hadn't come along. Some nights she would pack him off to bed and just cry herself to sleep. She knew thousands of other women had lost their men but to have him with her and just watch him slowly fall to pieces and fade away, well it was more than she could stand. She wished sometimes his pain and suffering could be ended, it seemed to her he would have been better-off being done for completely when the shell landed, instead of patched-up and brought back to life. This was no life, not for him, not for her.

The few months that Sam was with them took her out of herself, although she was never unfaithful to Fred. Despite everything she still loved him. He was the man she married. For better or worse, for richer or poorer, in sickness and in health, till death us do part. No, even though she'd had a bad time of it these last few years, and even though she liked it when Sam was around, she couldn't do that to Fred. Not that Sam would have wanted it any other way. He saw too many of his comrades shot and injured in the war, blown up, horrifically burnt, maimed and scarred; no, he stayed at the Cavendish Arms as much for Fred as he did for anyone else. About a month after he had left, Sam was living down in Marun St.Davids with his old friend Walter who owned a fishing-boat, and was beginning to plan where he would spend the Winter. He hadn't made it far enough to go to his usual winter quarters near Newquay, so he'd started to look for somewhere else. September was well under way and as soon as October arrived the nights would start to get colder again. On a particularly dark and dismal day Sam and his mate were sitting in the small fishermans café on the quayside playing dominoes to pass the time. They hadn't put to sea that morning as the forecast was bad so had to content themselves with the company of others. Then it happened, Mrs Henderson walked in, Sam spotted her straightaway and called her over. By now it was pouring with rain, and she was soaked.

"Come and sit by the fire," he said softly to her, beckoning her over to the small one-bar electric fire by their table. He could see she wasn't in the mood for his usual rumbustious approach. As she sat there warming up, he got the cook to make her a cup of tea and as she slowly drank, he asked her what she was doing there. "I've been searching for you for a couple of days," she said between sips, "I remembered you telling me about a fisherman friend that you always stay with down near Fowey, but I couldn't remember exactly where." Tears welled up in her eyes, "I just knew if I called into the pubs and cafés along the coast a-ways I would eventually find you." She looked straight at him, "Fred's dead."

She turned away and stared out through the rain-washed windows across the quay, sipped some more tea and cradled the empty cup in her hands. Sam put his arm around her and cuddled her.

"Well, you found me now, old girl," he said softly.

"He went barely two weeks after you'd gone" she continued, "and these past few weeks since then have been terrible."

"Look my lovely," he said, "why don't I get my things together and we'll take you back home." She looked up at him. "I'll stay with you for a while, if you'll have me," he added. It was what she'd wanted to hear, and it brought a tiny smile of relief to her face.

"Of course I will, you daft old pudding, why do you think I've come all this way looking for you."

They spent the entire winter together after that. They didn't start to sleep with each other straight away, it was a gradual process. They sort of grew fonder and fonder of each other as the months went by. She hadn't had much of a romantic time with her late husband for several years now and she found the love of a man was something she'd missed. The first time they went together it caught both of them by surprise. When it was over they both lay quite still in the dark, neither of them spoke, Sam could hear her breathing softly, "all right my lovely?"

"Yes" she replied quietly, "... I think I might have fallen in love with you Sam ..." and with that they both cuddled a bit more and slowly fell to sleep.

It was later in the New Year and the pub had all been dressed up for Valentine's Night and they'd had such a good evening that when it was closing time, they sort of fell into each other's arms. Sam had sung *Barbara Allen* to her for the first time, and she just wanted to hold him, to have him with her, she didn't want to be alone anymore. Of course, Sam being Sam, as soon as Spring arrived, he would start to get the wanderlust again. She understood. He was a roamer, and it would be cruel to expect him to change, to tie him down. But she would miss him. He'd gotten her over a bad patch in her life and she would always be thankful. They would see each other in the coming years, she knew that, and she would always have something to look forward to. But it would never be a permanent arrangement.

When they finished the bath Sam wrapped a towel round himself and began combing his hair and tidying his beard in front of the half-steamed bathroom mirror. He wanted to make himself look as presentable as possible. Barbara slipped her dressing-gown back on and disappeared into the bedroom. There's something alluring and comforting about having a hot bath with someone. The lovely warm feeling you get all over your body, and the intimacy of laying in the water naked together lasts for hours. You go to bed feeling all aglow with your skin all tingling and fresh. So it was with Sam and Barbara. They went to bed. The warmth and affection between two people who love each other is something they'd both missed but never realised how much.

In the still of the night, she found herself awake and sitting up in bed, just looking. Looking at Sam and wondering. Wondering how she was going to tell him. If only she could have found the courage to have asked him to stay with her on his last visit, then they could have had the last three years or so with each other as well. She began to dream about how it might have been. Pretty soon she laid back down, snuggled up to Sam and fell contentedly back to sleep. In the morning, they made breakfast for each other. She put on the bacon and eggs and Sam made the tea.

"How about some fried bread?" he asked.

"For you my old Romany - anything," and she flashed him that captivating smile which had first attracted him to her. She was wonderful. In her late forties' with a neat trim figure, shapely legs and lovely delicate features. She had that rare beauty which seemed to shine through the gloom when she smiled, Sam often wondered why she found him so appealing, after all, in his eyes he wasn't much of a catch. It often flummoxed him. On his travels he would sometimes sit and read back through his journal. Every time he got back to where his roaming took him through Barbara's world there were always bigger entries, more memories, wonderful remembrances. It never failed to amaze him how she would just take up with him, there and then, without any queries or questioning. He always worried that one day she'd see him for what he was, a fat old goat with a curly mop and a beard to match, but she never did. He loved her for that. He should have married her, but then, he could never have given her what she wanted, what he thought she wanted at any rate. A stable life and a husband to match. He wasn't the stay-at-home kind, so that was that.

"I know," she suddenly said, which broke his daydreaming, "let's go to the pictures."

"When?"

"This evening, I'll take the night off. There's a new Norman Wisdom film, '*The Square Peg*' on at the Plaza in the High Street."

"Who'll look after the pub?"

"I'll leave Rusty in charge - she can manage."

"Is she the ginger-haired one with the big hairdo? She gave me the come-on last night."

"Oh, she does that to everybody, the customers love it."

"Fair made me choke on my beer, young slip of a girl like that."

Barbara laughed, "that's settled then, we'll go to the pictures tonight. I haven't been out for ages, think I'll have my hair done, what do you think?" and with that she flung her head back with a mock swish to her hair as if to demonstrate a new style with a flourish of her blond locks. So, it was settled. They'd open the pub for the morning trade and then after lunch she'd go and have her hair done. And Sam could go to the barbers', seeing as how he had nothing better to do. It would only cost a few shillings and would probably take years off him she said. Well, you can't go wrong with a Norman Wisdom film. They laughed their heads off. It was the one where he's a road-worker digging a hole outside an army barracks and keeps shouting marching orders at the squaddies square-bashing inside. Well of course he gets drafted into the same barracks and before you know it he's digging-up roads over in France. Only being Norman he's three miles inside enemy lines and wouldn't you know it, he's the spitting-image of the local German Commandant. A square peg in a round hole. Just like Sam really, 'a bloke wot' lives everywhere and comes from nowhere' as his mate Nobby used to say.

Over the next few days they both worked in the pub, Sam helping out behind the bar, singing songs and cracking jokes with the regulars, and Barbara lording it over everybody like a queen bee over her drones. Life was good. It was like old times. It was a pity it wouldn't last, that this would be the last time he'd ever see her again. She didn't know how she was going to tell him; just find the right time and come straight out with it maybe? It wasn't as if they were married, hitched up together, inseparable. They were both adults. She was sure he'd understand. Still, not worth spoiling things just at the moment, may as well leave things as they were for the time-being and see how it went over the next few days.

"You've been here a week today," she said to him one morning over breakfast.

"Doesn't time fly when you're having fun," he grinned back at her.

"Have you enjoyed yourself?" she asked, not really needing an answer.

"As much as I ever could have wished," he gently took hold of her hand across the kitchen table, "it's been lovely" he said, and squeezed it softly, "on all of my travels this is one of my most favourite stopping places."

This wasn't a good time to tell him then. Never mind, there was bound to be another opportunity. She decided it best to just enjoy the moment and tell him later. "Fancy a picnic on Sunday?" she asked as they washed-up the dishes, "we could go up over the moor to Fenton, it's pretty over by there."

Sam hadn't heard of it but nodded his approval whilst at the same time whistling a tune to himself as he worked. Sunday came and they opened the pub as usual for the traditional Drink before the old Sunday Roast brigade and as luck would have it the sun came out. The weather was really warming up now, Summer was a'coming, and it would be a belter' according to Sam and his bits of dried seaweed. Not only that but the strawberries had arrived earlier this year too. He could feel it in his water, it was definitely gonna' be a belter'. So convinced was he that they went for a picnic in just their shirtsleeves. Figuratively speaking of course. Barbara had asked Rusty and the other girls to get a shifty-on at closing-time while she made some egg sandwiches, then when everywhere was done she and Sam could 'make a quick exit'. Bombing along - if you could call it that - in Fred's old grey Standard they soon got on their way. Barbara was pleased she'd learnt to drive after the War. She had to really, what with Fred's injuries, someone had to do all the running about. Going to the wholesalers', popping into the market for fresh veg' every day, that sort of thing. She found it quite a treat. In fact, once, she even had to call out an AA Man when she broke down going over to Cordingley, and was chuffed to bits when he pulled-up on his bright yellow motorcycle, gave her a salute and asked; 'Can I be of assistance Madam?' It made her feel really good. An independent woman. That's what the car gave her, independence. Like this afternoon on the picnic to Fenton with Sam.

He could drive, he learnt how to in the war, but the roads were so fast and furious it didn't appeal to him anymore. He preferred to walk. Not that the traffic was really that fast or that furious. Barbara never got over forty'... It was just Sam, stuck in his ways as usual and thinking that the world was getting faster and faster all the time. It wasn't. Not really. It was probably him getting slower and slower if the truth were known. You can't halt progress you just have to go with the flow.

Or drop out, like Sam.

Or like Barbara.

Fenton was pretty. Sam wondered why he'd never come across it before in his travels; he decided it was because he always stuck to the coast-roads when he came Westwards. Which was a shame because there were probably dozens of other little places inland a-ways like this that he'd missed out on. The river that meandered its way up from Mapleton had by now shrunk to not much more than a wide shallow stream, a bit muddy looking but pleasant enough, and Barbara and Sam were camped out on the banks with their picnic. Sandwiches, crisps, salted peanuts and some bottles of light-ale with two glasses from the pub. Sam had taken his shirt off and was laying down on the cover, sunbathing. Barbara was laying by the side of him wishing she could take her shirt off too.

"In the future," she said, "I'll bet women'll take their tops off on the beaches and what-have-you to sunbathe, and nobody will take a blind bit of notice..."

"I dunno' about that," Sam replied with a smile "if you had your breasts out now, I couldn't help but notice - and a right nice sight they'd make too!" and he leaned over and gave her a big kiss.

"Yes, but it's not fair, look at you with your shirt off without a care in the world, if I did that I'd be ogled and pointed at" she continued, "and I'm just as hot as you are..."

"I expect you are my lovely and I'd love to see you take your shirt off, blouse off, whatever it is, but you'd get us arrested" and he kissed her again and laughed.

"Still," she added "I suppose I'd better get used to the heat, considering where I'm going."

At first Sam didn't twig what she had said, and then slowly it dawned on him, and he asked her gingerly, "where's that then?"

She rolled on to her side so that she could speak to him face-to-face. "I'm off to Australia in six weeks" she said, "I'm emigrating." She looked into Sam's face and noticed a sadness forming deep within his eyes as the news sunk in. She gently stroked her hand across his shoulders and down along his arm, finally reaching the fingers of his hand which she held softly. "It'll be alright," she said, "you'll get over me."

He looked sorrowfully at her, "I'll never get over you... my beautiful Devon girl."

They didn't say much after that, Barbara rolled back-over onto her back and Sam did the same. They both lay quietly with their thoughts. High overhead a lone skylark sang out its territorial song and then plummeted to the ground in that death defying drop that they do to avoid predators finding their nests. Minutes later it was back on high, singing away, and then it was ready to drop all over again. Sam spoke as he lay there watching and listening.

"Of course, it's all a ruse you know - the skylark - all that dropping and falling. They do it to confuse their enemies," he softly said. Barbara lay silently and listened. "When they actually land on the ground, it's nowhere near where their nest is, it's a trick. They land in one place and then run along the ground to another place where their nest really is, that way, nobody will find it. That's the plan anyway..." He paused, "bit like us really - Humans - We fall in love for all the world to see, singing on high, and then when it's all over we drop. We try to hide ourselves, our sorrows, try not to let it show, but it's there all the same, hidden..." She held his hand.

"Soppy old sod," she said "you only ever see me from one journey to the next, anybody would think we were childhood sweethearts, couldn't bear to be parted from each other. And anyway -" she sat up and leaned with her arms across his chest, "you must have women all over the country, good looking feller' like you with all your little stopping-off places. I can't be the only bit of spice in your life."

"I have to confess," he started, "that as far as I can recall, you are my one and only distraction." She whacked him on the arm.

"Sauce!" she said, all indignantly, "just for that you can sleep on the sofa tonight." He laughed at the thought of it, smiled lovingly at her and gave her a kiss, wrapped both arms around her pert body and gave her a bear-hug.

"That's right" she said with the wind squeezed out of her "kill me off as well why don't you?" and laughed back at him.

That's how they stayed for a good quarter-of-an-hour, her on top of him, leaning on his chest. Him holding her tightly so as to savour every moment, feel every curve and crevice as her body rose and fell rhythmically with his every breath; and all the while kissing and necking and whispering sweet nothings to each other.

"Lay down with me..." she said softly, "right here - right now...".

He sat up, looked around to see if the coast was clear, "are you sure?"

"'Course I am, I wouldn't have asked otherwise. Come on..." she said, "nobody will see us, not laying on this grassy bank" and rolled over onto the blanket and gave him that look with her eyes that says, 'here I am, come and make love to me'. The trouble with doing it in the open was that anything could happen. Someone could suddenly stumble across the scene innocently out walking their dog. You could get stung on the backside by a bee. It could rain! Anything! As it happened, they could never have guessed what was about to occur.

Occasionally lifting his head to see if anyone was coming, they were both trying to concentrate and enjoy the moment, all soft and warm with the Sun beating down, but in the circumstances not making a very good job of it.

It didn't help with Barbara laughing, "hurry up," she said, "or we might get caught." It was like being a teenager all over again, having a bit of hanky-panky in a corn field or behind the bike-sheds, all fingers and thumbs, fumbling about trying to undo her bra-straps, trying not to ladder her stockings and not really getting anywhere. Trying his hardest to focus himself and not be affected by it all, Sam shut his mind to the outside world and the laughter and the worry of being caught '*in flagrante*' and just enjoyed the loveliness of this beautiful day and the two of them entwined in a loving embrace.

Unfortunately for Sam, he'd only been looking ahead and to the sides, completely ignoring the river behind them. Which was rather disastrous because it was about that time in the early evening when the cows come in for milking, and like clockwork they merrily make their way across the fields. And along the riverbanks. Well, he got the shock of his life. All of a sudden, and whilst he'd been particularly deep in concentration, he jumped-up with a start as a jet of steaming hot air wafted out of the nostrils of a Jersey crossbreed straight up the crack of his bare buttocks!!!

"Jesus Christ!" he exclaimed loudly, and quickly hoisted up his trousers, "a herd of bloody cows...".

Laugh, Barbara couldn't stop herself. There they were, deep in the throes of passion, all alone and oblivious to the world around them, then along comes this herd of cows, nosy as ever: 'coo, look at that ladies, let's go and have a look over by there, see what's goin' on...' you could almost imagine them saying.

Sam was up now and trying to shoo' them away, Barbara was buttoning her top back up, readjusting herself, straightening herself out, and all the while breaking out in uncontrollable fits of laughter. Quite what the farmhand (who wandered by a few minutes later) thought of it all was anybody's guess... After a moment or two Sam managed to move the cows on, sat back down on the blanket, looked at Barbara and laughed. This would definitely be a story for his journal, he'd remember this one for a long time. It made a better-than-expected end to a day which might have turned quite sour, what with Barbara's shock announcement. That evening in the pub one of the barmaids innocently asked, 'if they'd had a pleasant day out today'. They just burst out laughing and the poor young girl mumbled to herself, 'What have I said?' as they both turned and walked away unable to control themselves.

The next few days things carried on as before with Sam and Barbara enjoying themselves in the bar each day and then in the flat upstairs each night but they both knew it had to end. Barbara had explained how things sometimes got too much for her, running the pub and all; and how the town seemed to be changing. Seemed to be growing bigger all the time, attracting a certain breed of people - overspill from the bigger places along the coast probably. There had been trouble in the pub some nights, fights and what-have-you, which were unheard of even just a few years ago. The Brewery sometimes made her life difficult. A lone woman in charge of a growing town-pub; she should really have a man about the place, for security and so on. They were right of course and although she was always pleased to see Sam, he was never going to be a permanent fixture. Both her son and her daughter had emigrated to Australia some years before and were beginning to make new lives for themselves. Her daughter had a baby on the way, and she couldn't bear the thought of never seeing her first grandchild. There was nothing keeping her here, Fred had been gone several years now and apart from Sam, there was no one else. He understood.

It must have been hard for her, what with him just flitting in and out of her life the way he did. It was a bit of luck he'd come this way now though; another summer and it would have been too late she would have been gone. Although she had about six weeks to go before sailing Sam thought it best not to hang around until the bitter end. He told her one evening as they lay in bed together sipping a late-night cup of cocoa.

She'd be sorry to see him go but, in the circumstances, thought it was better to break now, rather than later. "Besides," she said, "there's a lot to do before I go, sort out my belongings, sell the car, hand over the pub" - he interrupted her,

"cancel the milk,"

" - and I'd get on a lot better if I didn't have a great lummox like you loafing about the place, getting under my feet, singing songs to me all the time."

"And taking you to bed" he added.

"Yes, and taking me to bed" she repeated softly, giving him a cuddle. She kissed him, "I shall miss you Sam, you got me through some bad times one way and another, and I'll never forget that, but life moves on."

"Just like me my lovely - always moving on."

Two days later Sam was gone. Barbara would never see him again. He'd written out the words of *Barbara Allen* for her to remember him by and decorated it with tiny cartoon drawings of Jersey crossbreed cows. She'd given him her son's address in Adelaide in case he ever felt like writing to her, and a small silver locket with her photograph inside it.

He'd never forget Barbara Henderson.

Never.

Chapter 6

Built like a brick sh*t-house

Sleeping in the outdoors on a warm summers' evening was something that Sam always loved to do. Mind you he'd not done much of it these past few weeks, so he was glad to get back into it: well maybe not glad for the reason behind it, but never-the-less glad to be doing it. Under the stars with nothing but the Heavens and the creatures of the night for company was quite a humbling experience especially if a beautiful strawberry moon shone out all bright and clear. He was quite a solitary figure, really, even though he could readily enjoy himself in the company of others, so it was never his thing in life to be part of it all, never his reason to be. It wouldn't bother him if he didn't see another soul for weeks on end. He could just as easily talk to the trees or the animals; or the empty piece of space three feet in front of him, whenever he found himself talking to himself.

Which he often did.

The trouble with talking to an empty piece of space three in front of you was that if other folk saw you doing it they nearly always thought you were crackers, which you probably were. Unless you were a bloke called Sam. "A bloke -"said Sam to his three feet of space as he trod his way along the line of a furrow in a freshly ploughed field, "what a strange word – bloke - I wonder where it comes from?" Ever one to increase his knowledge of all things useless, thought-worthy and philosophical, he often came out with these pronouncements. Usually, it heralded a stop for a brew-up somewhere up ahead and today was no exception. You could pretend that you had something really deep and meaningful to contemplate and a cup of tea was just the right source of inspiration you would need to do it justice.

Not wishing to simply traipse straight across the middle of this particular newly ploughed field though he'd decided to walk the way it led him, the way the tractor' had taken cutting its furrows, and just see where it would go. It was one of those huge wide-open modern fields where all the little dividing intersections had been done away with by the wanton removal of the hedgerows. So big that it followed the undulations of the surrounding countryside and disappeared up over a hill and out of sight. With no particular end in view Sam was therefore content to just keep walking in a straight line in the vee' of the ploughed soil.

"A bloke named Pete - had smelly feet, and smelly armpits too," he began as he decided to try and make-up a nonsense rhyme, "he had false-teeth and a wooden leg - and hair that was stuck with glue" he laughed out loud and startled a pheasant. Up it sparked not ten feet from where he was walking and made that loud cack-cack-cack sound as it flew off at high speed across the dark red soil of the field. A shot rang out which startled Sam and as he watched he half expected to see the bird stopped dead in its tracks and plummet to the ground in a spray of feathers, all its grace and beauty gone in an instant. But no, it carried on as before elegantly and swiftly making its escape from nothing more sinister than Sam's belly laugh. He turned slowly to look all about him, scanning the horizon as he did so, but could see no huntsman, no shotgun wielding farmer out for a day's sport, and wondered where the shot could have come from.

He carried on walking and could at last see the edge of the field and made his way toward it. A cup of tea was a definite must; he was intrigued by the situation and wanted to stop and sit a while to ponder on it. 'A shot with no shooter'. In the meantime, as he covered the last few hundred yards, he went back to his notion of the origin of the word 'bloke'.

"P'raps it comes from bullock" he thought to himself "and got corrupted down the ages as meaning a male animal who can be relied on..." 'A good bullock's worth 'avin" he'd heard many a farmer say, although he couldn't think why, seeing as how it was not much use for anything - except pulling a cart maybe. So that was it then, he'd decided.

The word bloke came from the word bullock, that was another one settled.

In the quarter of an hour that it had taken him to reach the other side of the field and get his billy-can kettle on, he heard the gunshot another three times and each time could see no one around pulling the trigger. 'It's a mystery and no mistake' he said to himself as he sat on a clump sipping his mug of tea; then he spotted it. Far away across to the far side of the field he suddenly noticed a little puff of smoke about two feet above the ground and a split second later heard the bang of another 'mystery shot'.

"Morning..." said a voice out of the blue, "wot'chew doin' bye there?" Sam turned and saw a young man in black wellingtons and brown mole-skin trousers standing twenty or so feet behind him, obviously the farmer's son, and carrying what looked to be a kind of rolled-up hessian rope slung over the shoulders of his donkey-jacket.

"Having a cup of tea lad." Sam stood as he spoke and beckoned the young man over "come and join me."

"Don't mind if I do, I been walking these fields all mornin' an' my feet are fair killin' me" he replied and sat himself down next to Sam and graciously took the tin-mug of tea being offered to him, "lovely" he swooned as he drank, "'ot an' sweet - just 'ow I likes it."

"My name's Sam. Do you live round these parts?"

"Arr, up over the top by there, Johnsons Farm, that's my dad's place, Ephraim Johnson. This is me dad's land you're sittin' on. My name's Joseph. People round 'ere call me Jake."

"Pleased to meet you, Jake." Just then another shot rang out. Jake didn't take a blind bit of notice. They sat talking and drinking, Sam asked if there was any work going on his dad's farm, but Jake replied that as he had four brothers and two sisters there was more than enough of them to manage. He could try over the other way 'about 'alf-a-mile up over the top in Fossey Woods, they were doing some clearing over that way and could "mebbe' do wi' another pair of hands - just follow the dogs, you can't miss it."

Just then another shot rang out to which Jake retorted "bugger, that's the last one. I'll 'ave to be off old timer, me scarer's 'ave run out" and with that he stood up and sloped off in the direction of the puff of smoke. As he walked away, he carried on talking back to Sam, explaining that they'd spread a dose of potash salts out yesterday and were trying to keep the birds an' such off for a while, keep em' safe, and the bangers was the only way of frightenin' 'em away. It wouldn't 'arm 'em, but they was trying anyway - just in case. As he passed further out of ear-shot Sam could just make-out the remnants of his conversation "if you'me just walked across't this field I should give them boots o' yours a good scrub if'n I were you..." and he finally got too far away to hear anymore. Sam waved an arm to signal that he'd heard and glanced down at them. Sure enough, they were encrusted with mud and sticking to it was a sheen of white crystallized 'dust', obviously the potash powder which Jake had referred to.

Packing his things he began the half mile walk to Fossey Woods, via a puddle or two in which to rinse his boots off. As he topped the rise, he could see the woods below quite clearly and made his way there. In the open countryside a half-a-mile isn't really that far and probably would only take a few minutes to walk. He whistled 'Greensleeves' to himself. Bang! Jake had started up again.

Walking into the perimeter of Fossey Woods Sam could indeed hear some dogs, along with other general sounds and noises. He'd deviated a little from his normal coast roads the last few days, not feeling too enthusiastic for the sights and sounds of the sea since leaving Mapleton and had found himself a little more in-land than he'd previously been. The sound of work was getting nearer, an axe chopping away methodically; a chainsaw; the twisting tearing crunching sound of a tree being felled. All manner of things. Trouble was in the dense cover you couldn't really make out which direction it was coming from, best to keep walking dead ahead. He was obviously getting closer as the sounds gradually became louder, including the dogs.

Just then slap bang in front of him were two huge brown Irish wolfhounds, teeth bared and jaws slavering, with their ears pricked, their eyes wild and their shackles standing so high you could have given them a crew-cut. There they stood, all three just staring at each other. Bang! One of Jake's scarers sounded off in the distance. They didn't flinch. These two were true hunting dogs, trained not to be jumped by the sound of gunshot. And trained in their especially silent creeping way of coming up on their prey unexpectedly like a pair of lurchers. That was the thing with lurchers, if they were good at their job, you shouldn't be able to hear them coming, bred as a silent hunting-dog. And these two were good.

Sam had stood stock still, frozen in his tracks for what seemed like several minutes but was probably only mere seconds, just to get the measure of them, decide what to do next. No use taking any chances. In that uncanny way that he had of communing with animals, whether it be foxes or sheep, cows or horses, he quietly and carefully knelt to the ground, slipped his rucksack off his shoulder and started talking to the two dogs. It was always his reasoning that to communicate with God's creatures you had to get onto their level. No use standing there at your full height expecting to be able to put your hand out in welcome and not get it bitten off, that would be crazy; and these two were quite capable of doing that kind of damage. Far better to approach them low and slow. It was a bit like a grizzly bear Sam had read about once, in a Davy Crockett story or somewhere, they always stand fully upright to get an advantage over their attackers - make themselves appear huge and formidable - which was the last thing Sam wanted to do with these two... He didn't want to come across as a huge six-foot two brown beast and challenge them to a duel or anything. Much better to come across as a friend, someone to trust, someone not to kill...

The plan worked. Within a few minutes he'd forged a strange ethereal bond with the two animals and was calming them down from their crazed anger. The teeth disappeared, the drool stopped slavering, and their haunches softened and became less tense. It was working.

"You alright Mister?" came a voice from a thicket. A young boy, probably thirteen or fourteen came into view, "sorry about those two, me dad said they'd gone too quiet, that they were up to no good, so he sent me to fetch 'em." At the appearance of their young master the two animals' behaviour changed completely, which relieved Sam. He'd often worried that his so-called affinity with other animals might desert him one day, just when he might need it most, and these two were a test of that premise, but no, he had made friends (of sorts) so he was pleased he hadn't lost his touch. Picking up his belongings he spoke to the young boy, somewhat gruffly. "These two belong to you?"

It was lucky that it was Sam who had happened along, anybody else being confronted by two ferocious hunting dogs might not have been so quick thinking as him and the consequences didn't bear thinking about. "They won't 'urt you, me dad says they're all mouth and no trousers, just a couple of soppy windbags who like to play at being tough." Which might have been true, considering the change in the two of them since the boy arrived. They did seem to be two totally different animals in his company, playful even. "They likes you" he said, patting and fussing the two of them. Having made friends with both the dogs and the lad, Sam thought it worth venturing further as to the chance of any work, "your dad got any work for a travelling man?"

"You a gypsy Mister?"

"No, 'fraid not."

"It's just me dad say's these two are gypsy dogs an' I wondered if that's why they didn't go for you. My dad's allus' got work, more'n 'ee can 'andle, over this way Mister," and with that the lad whistled loudly, set the dogs off ahead of him, turned and clambered back through the thicket to where his father and the others were working. Sam followed. Bang!

In the clearing he could see three men hard at work, the two dogs already back at play having run ahead of himself and the boy. As they approached the older of the men looked across at Sam and smiled, "them dogs didn't get you then..." he was a short, stocky, well-built man in his middle forties with good strong arms and a jolly smile.

"No, it was fine, more noise than anything," replied Sam as pleasantly as possible, given that for two pins he could have easily ended-up clubbing both animals about the head with the nearest lump of wood if they had have started anything; but he didn't want to get off on the wrong foot with their owner so played it cool.

" 'ass alright then."

"He wants some work dad," piped in the young boy eagerly. He'd taken an instant liking to Sam and wanted him to stay awhile.

" 'ass fine by me Jonas - fine by me."

"I can do most things, well, anything really," added Sam, keeping up the young boy's enthusiasm, "and I'm cheap," he added with a smile.

"Righto my old cod-fish - we're clearing the scrub out to give the saplin's a bit more light, loppin' the odd tree. Six pound a week cash-in-hand an' lunch wi' me an' the boys on the 'ouse. Me name's Sam," and the woodsman put out his hand in welcome. Sam shook it vigorously, he always figured a good strong handshake was the measure of a man; you could tell a lot by the way someone shook your hand and as first impressions always counted the most, he got in good and strong every time.

"Er - my name is Sam as well," he said, and smiled.

"Well bugger me," said Sam the Woodsman, and laughed.

"We'll 'ave to call you Big Sam then," one of the two men jibed, "on account of you're built like a brick shithouse an' 'ee's built like a piddlin' squirt... no offence Boss." Big Sam laughed. Woodsman Sam went a strange shade of pinky red, and his young son Jonas laughed his head off at the thought of it. It seemed a good a time as any to stop for a break. Bang!

As the days were lovely and long with Summer well on its way no one was in any particular hurry to finish for the day. With no watch to tell him the time

Sam had decided it best not to worry and just work until the others did. Stop when they stopped. After all, six pounds a week with a free lunch wasn't half bad and to be honest he could do with the money as his reserve-tin was only hiding a few coppers, and a couple of ha'pennies. When it was finally time to call it a day Little Sam stood up, straightened his aching back, scratched his head, looked at his pocket-watch and announced, "that'll do lads - 'alf past seven, pub's been open more'n an hour now - let's pack it in for today."

"You got somewhere to sleep tonight Big Sam?" said one of the other woodcutters as they strolled off through the trees together and out into the open fields.

"No, I usually sleep under the stars or in a cowshed or hayrick, wherever, I'm easy," replied Sam as they walked along.

"Nothin' like that round 'ere."

"No matter, I can soon rustle-up a bivvy back there in the clearing, it doesn't bother me."

"What about the pub?" remarked Little Sam.

"Oh, I'll not miss that," replied Sam, "I like a few pints after a hard day's graft, and besides," he added "I'm famished" and clapped one of the men across the shoulders in that friendly manner of his to fair knock the wind right out of him. "Any chance of a sub' Boss?" he quickly added, "only I'm a bit short..." they all laughed.

Jonas caught up with the two men as they all made their way down the track and towards the small village pub. Bang! It was no good, he'd have to ask, that noise had been going off all day long and it still puzzled him. “Jonas, lad, what's that gunshot sound I've been hearing today?”

The young boy looked up and laughed, “It's me dad's bangers. 'Ee makes 'em for ol' man Johnson - ”

“That's Farmer Johnson to you my boy,” piped up Little Sam away in front of them.

“Me dad sometimes 'as to use dynamite to clear an old stump when it can't be got out by a tractor or digger', so 'ee allus' 'as gunpowder an' stuff lyin' about the place. Anyhow 'ee twines-up these 'ome-made bangers into this hessian rope see, an' adds a bit of potassium nitrate along the way as 'ee's goin'.”

“And that way,” said Little Sam interrupting his son's story, “I can get the bang to go off at reg'lar intervals while the rope burns.”

“Sort of like a slow fuse” added Sam.

“Yeh - but better. You just counts off as many bangs as you needs through the day, cut the rope to length, string 'em up to a pole some-wheres an' light the end.”

Jonas interrupted his father, “yeh, my mate Jake sets 'em out, 'ee lights the end of 'is rope an' it just sort of smoulders along all day, settin' off the bangs one at a time till they're all gone” the boy excitedly added to the story, running along by the side of them so as to keep up with Sam's strident pace.

So that explained why they were so regular and why the puff of smoke had appeared to be two feet above the ground. “So that's what the rope was hanging around Jake's neck,” added Sam, saying that he'd met him earlier that day and they'd shared a cup of tea. “It was Jake that sent me to you when I asked about work hereabouts.”

“Well good on 'im” said Little Sam as they finally came to the village and walked into the Huntsman's

Arms. "Four pints o' mild an' 'alf a cider for the boy please Moira," he said as they approached the bar, "an' get this man some grub, 'ee must be fair starvin' a great big fella like that," and slapped a five-pound note down onto the bar with the intention of paying for all of it himself, no mention of the sub. Sam appreciated the gesture. He'd tried to make a good impression during the day and had worked particularly hard, it had obviously been noticed. "An' give us a bottle o' stout each for the dogs, will you Moira love, they'm be fair gagging o' thirst" he said, "an' better give them some dinner an' all" he added. "Wotch'you got?"

Moira looked at him across the bar, "you know what I got Sam Morley, the same as I've always got, you old bugger" she said and smiled, "beef n' onion pasty or pork n' apple pie - you takes it or you leaves it" she said.

"Such a lovely lass," he said quietly behind his hand to Sam, "such a way wi' words, but I still loves 'er."

Sam knew what it was to love a pub landlady. The other two woodsmen, Pete and Mike, were both married so didn't stay for any food as they would both have had hot dinners waiting for them back at home, but it didn't stop them downing a couple of pints each before they left. Well, they had worked quite hard today as well so probably deserved it. Sam wondered why Jonas and his dad didn't seem to be in any hurry to get home as they ordered the food. Soon all three of them were wolfing down Moira's home-made cooking and delicious it was too. Sam had chosen the pork as it 'made a nice change.' You got fed up eating beef all the time back then and now and again it was good to have something different.

He couldn't remember the last time he'd seen a plump juicy roast chicken on a pub menu for a Sunday dinner treat, still there'd probably come a time when chicken was ten-a-penny and beef would be the luxury, what with these new factory farming methods he kept hearing about.

When they'd finished eating Jonas went to the bar and ordered another round of drinks, two pints of mild for the two Sam's, two bottles of stout for the two dogs and half a cider for himself.

A voice came out from across the pub. "Is that boy old enough?" said the voice of the person sitting in the corner by the log fire, playing draughts.

"Course 'e is Constable Melcombe," called out Little Sam "'e 'll be fourteen next birthday."

"That's alright then" answered the policeman, "just checking," and smiled.

Sam spluttered into his beer glass as he downed the last remaining inch of ale ready for the fresh one to be poured in. Woodsman Sam looked at him and winked, "take no notice of 'im, the old fart, it's only me cousin Donald Melcombe and a right prat 'e is too" and laughed. " 'Eee's a policeman - black sheep of the family."

By the time they'd drank their last pint Sam noticed young Jonas dozing off quietly against the bench seat arm-rest and that the two dogs were themselves all but in the land of nod. Their fat bodies lolloped out across the floor so that anyone wishing to get by had to step gingerly in between their outstretched limbs, trying not to tread on them. Not that the dogs themselves would have done anything about it if somebody had tried to get past them, with a belly full of stout and a large helping of beef stew they were too content to bother. As were the three humans. A good meal and a quart of ale was enough to send any man into a sleepy stupor.

"S'pose we ought to be makin' a move" said Little Sam "the boy's fair whacked out" he added, lifting Jonas up off the seat. "Where you stayin' tonight Samuel?"

"Do you know - I'd forgotten all about that!" Sam answered in exclamation.

"Well, that's settled then, you'm can sleep in our place - foller me" and with that he nudged Jonas awake, kicked the two dogs playfully to arouse them as well, kissed Moira goodnight and made his exit through the pub and out the back door passing the Gents toilets on the way. Like a shambolic entourage the rest of them followed him out in single file, each one receiving a goodnight kiss from Moira. Well, the dogs got a pat on the head, you couldn't really kiss a huge great ten stone hunting dog, even if it was half asleep, and of course Sam, even though he was a huge great seventeen stone giant of a man got a kiss. At least he wouldn't try and bite her head off.

Walking from the light of the bar into the gloomy darkness of the backyard of the pub it took a few minutes for Sam's eyes to adjust but he could have sworn they were walking towards a railway train.

Their home was a shambles. A higgeldy-piggeldy heap. It was what you would expect of two men living in such small confines, they did their best but without a wife for Little Sam and a mother for Jonas it wasn't easy. The sort of shambles you wouldn't mind living in though because it was a nice shambles. Not dirty. Just untidy. Piles of old newspapers stacked here and there, Daily Telegraphs it looked like to Sam, big pages anyway. A stuffed owl fixed to a log perch, its gaze permanently fixed forward all glassy eyed and staring intensely. A budgie sat in its cage, twittering away, right by the side of the owl, 'to keep it company' according to Little Sam. More than likely it was living in dread fear of being gobbled up by this fierce looking bird that lived by the side of it and did nothing but stare at it all day long, thought Sam to himself.

Above the mantle-piece was a big round clock, its face about twenty inches in diameter, with huge hands and enormous numerals, like a railway station clock, designed so that you could see it from a distance, rather than looking at it like now from just two feet away. Sam just prayed that it wasn't a chimer! Hanging on a wall, amongst a hundred other things hanging on the walls, pictures, family photographs, cuttings, film star portraits, messages about odd jobs that needed doing, notes about work that was still waiting to be done, was a three-foot-long, oblong glass cabinet with a stuffed and mounted pike proudly displayed inside it. The inscription read "*Reverend Gillespie 1842 - Wallbush Lake, Overcourt, 28lbs 4oz*" which was obviously the name of the captor, not the poor unfortunate fish that had given him his place in history, thus giving up its own life for the privilege. Immortalized forever as a murderer of fish, what an epitaph, "He caught a big fish once..."

Everywhere Sam looked he saw things; bottles, fossils, old Davy-lamps, some miners helmets, old boots, a crystal ball, a stuffed squirrel on a wooden plinth, all manner of flotsam and jetsam tumbled about amongst the furniture and shelves. In fact, the more he looked the more he realised that it was making his head spin, taking it all in, trying to assimilate his surroundings, and decided to give it up, go to bed and have another go in the morning. He would be fresher then, more alert. One thing that did catch his eye as he began to doze off lying on the 'chaze-longoo', as Little Sam had called it, was piles of money lying about the place. Shoe-boxes full of ten-shilling notes, one-pound notes and the odd five-pound note, various coins, half-crowns and so on stuffed in anywhere that was capable of holding it. An old fruit bowl, an empty goldfish bowl, a brown china teapot with the lid taken off so that the contents could be seen poking out the top. He'd never seen so much money! Perhaps Little Sam was one of those eccentric millionaires he'd read about once "got so much money they don't know what to do with it" he mused as he drifted off to sleep, "this house has got lots of windows too" he mumbled as his eyes finally gave up the ghost and closed softly sending him into the land of Nod as well.

In the morning, they were all up with the lark and after a quick wash in the "cloakroom" of the next carriage, along a corridor that used to be the First-Class compartments now turned into bedrooms and dining room and the like, they all five of them wandered across the courtyard into the back door of the pub where Moira was waiting. Two men, a sleepy-headed boy, and two dopey dogs. "It's a railway carriage," Sam said to himself as they stepped out into the cold morning light.

It was six o'clock in the morning and there she was standing at the stove cooking a huge fried breakfast of bacon, eggs, beans, tomatoes and mushrooms. She'd also sliced up some of last night left-over potatoes and was frying them in the chip pan. Even though it was early Sam was looking forward to it, he hadn't had a proper cooked breakfast for a few days, not since leaving Mapleton, and the smell was fair making his stomach grumble. And it would help to soak up last night's beer. She even fried some liver for the dogs, after they'd all had a bowl of porridge 'to keep you re'glar,' she'd said.

Half an hour later when they were all done Moira gave Jonas a thermos full of hot tea and a goodbye kiss as they went to leave. Sam tidied up the dirty plates into the sink and followed after him. 'Millionaire' Sam gave Moira a hug and a big kiss full on the lips "that was lovely my darlin'," he said, "you done us proud - why don't you go out today and treat yourself to somethin' new," and handed her a wad of money tightly rolled up with an elastic band. "Here's fifty pound my lovely, get somethin' nice." He turned to Sam with a big grin on his face and winked. "Let's be off."

Ahead of them Jonas was already climbing the stile over the fence and into the fields, with the two dogs running about him like huge overgrown puppies as they made their way towards the woods. About halfway across the other two woodsmen joined up with them, they too had a flask of tea each and all four men chatted as they walked amiably towards the clearing ready to start work at seven.

The air was lovely this time of day, the countryside was alive with birdsong and deep in the heart of the woods, out of sight from prying eyes, a lonely woodpecker could be heard hammering away at a tree trunk somewhere, looking for food or trying to make a home for itself. Although they'd had a good breakfast back at the pub they'd been working for a good three or four hours cutting back the hazel tines and clearing the debris and with Sam's appetite his huge bulk was in need of sustenance, so he was glad when Millionaire Sam called halt for a tea-break.

"Tea up!" he cheerfully shouted.

"About bluddy time too - me throat's parched" called back Mike. Pete, the other woodsman, strolled over to their small bivvy and got each men's flask out. Sam would have preferred a fresh brew-up, but he'd left all his cooking stuff back at the carriage. Still, beggars can't be choosers, and he should know. Thermos tea it would have to be, at least it was hot and sweet. What more could a man want? Well, something to eat would be nice.

Drinking the tea was fine but it only served to remind Sam's stomach that he hadn't eaten since six that morning and by now it must have been at least lunch time. Gurgle, rumble, gurgle, growl, rumble. It sounded as if two bears were having a fight in it. If only he had a watch on, he'd know whether or not it was anywhere near mid-day and if lunch was on the way or had already passed him by.

"That yourn stomach a'gurgling an' a'gaggling my ol' chip-butty' called out Millionaire Sam, laughing.

"Yes - sorry about that, but when I'm working, physical like, I works up quite fair old appetite. If I'm out on my own somewheres I usually stop whenever I want and cook something up."

"Well, no need, lunch 'll be about ten minutes. Pete's missus 'll be through 'ere soon on 'er 'orse an' she'll bring us all the grub we needs. Didn't I tell 'ee t'other day, lunch is on me..." It was true. He had said that. It was just that Sam hadn't seen any evidence of it. No one seemed to be carrying much with them first thing this morning, save the flasks, so he'd begun to worry. Couldn't go all day without food, not when you're working. No matter how big a breakfast he'd eaten.

"Can't let a big lad like you starve now can I," added Little Millionaire Sam with a wink.

"Must take at least 'alf a cow a'tween two bread vans to feed a bluddy great bloke like you" added Mike.

Sure enough, sometime after, Pete's wife rode up on an old pie-bald mare with a couple of bundles slung on each side of the saddle. When she had dismounted and untied the sacks Pete and Mike swiftly laid out the vittles she had brought. Truth be told they were probably hungry too, but didn't bother to say, knowing what was coming. Especially as Little Sam would have given them gyp about it once.

Trisha sat with her husband off to one side, quietly talking while they all sat and ate. She seemed somehow uneasy. Before she left, Little Sam walked over to them both. He kissed Trisha, just a little peck on the cheek as a thank-you, "lovely grub Trish, as always" and pushed a five-pound note into her coat pocket, "that's for you my dear - you done us proud again - and get them kids o' yours a lollipop each after school or something, my treat." She thanked him and looking up, smiled back at him, although she still seemed unsettled. Not her usual self. Tense. Little Sam, having a naturally non-judgemental attitude saw nothing in it, didn't even notice the slight nervousness in her voice when she accepted the money. He didn't even notice what her sad facial expression would have shown to anyone else. Sam noticed. He noticed that she wasn't quite right, even though he'd never met her before, he could tell at a glance that something was on her mind.

Living a life detached from society meant that he was in a good position to observe it. Looking in from the outside as it were. Being looked at but not being seen was a very handy phenomenon. It made him a good judge of character and while Pete's wife Trisha was obviously a bright young good-looking country girl at heart she was also under some kind of strain. In fact, after she'd gone, Pete himself seemed a bit strained. Suddenly he wasn't his usual self, not like he'd been so far this morning. She had brought him some news, clearly bad, at least that's what it seemed to Sam, when they had both sat quietly talking, almost whispering. He had thought of enquiring about it during the rest of the afternoon, but Pete didn't really make himself available for discussion, he seemed to be keeping himself to himself and he went straight home after work had finished, saying as how he didn't fancy a drink tonight thanks. Sam left it, after all he'd only just met them yesterday, so it was a bit too soon to be asking anyone intimate questions, so he felt it best to leave well alone.

At the pub that evening Sam was once again treated to some of Moira's home-made cooking, the pork and apple, which was delicious. Sort of sweet and yet spicy all at the same time, with just a hint of mustard to give it a twist. This carried on for the next few days with early morning breakfasts, working at the copse, having lunch in the clearing and then dinner at the pub until one evening, as they sat there drinking and eating, Sam noticed someone come into the bar and glance around at the occupants, as if looking for someone.

"Is there a Sam Morley, woodsman, of Morley & Son, in 'ere tonight?" enquired the stranger, "only I has to ask them about some tree work."

Little Sam beckoned the stranger over, stood up, held out an outstretched hand for a welcome handshake, burped unexpectedly, made everyone in the pub burst out laughing, embarrassed himself, went bright red, apologised, never made the welcome, sat back down again with a bump and said, "that'll be me you're after then." The beer and the food having just the wrong amount of soporific effect. Mike got a spare chair for the interloper. It seemed he worked on the big Estate over Chase Moor way, and they had some 'big elm trees with some kind of disease what needed to come down - and was he interested'.

"My boss says 'e 'll pay you fifty pounds, day after next, if you says yes," said the visitor.

"Tell 'im sixty pounds an' we'll be there tomorrow."

"Done," said the stranger.

"You certainly 'ave been," said Moira to herself under her breath as she walked over to their table with a fresh tray of drinks. The beer was soon shared out to the little huddle, the dogs with their stout, the boy with his cider, Sam with a pint of mild and the others with brown ale. After a few more drinks the stranger made arrangements for the morning, gave them directions as to how to find the place, bade them farewell and rode off into the night, his little Austin zigzagging down the unlit country lanes for all it was worth. "We'll be there at eight," called Little Sam after the car as it drove off into the night.

Back in the bar Moira was tidying things up, "sixty pounds!" she said out loud in disbelief to the four of them sitting there as Sam walked back into the pub, "you're a crook Sam Morley" she said, waving an empty beer glass at him.

"'oo me?" he replied, with that silly grin of his "never. If'n that feller wants to offer me fifty pounds just to cut down a few trees then that's 'is lookout, so I reckon sixty is even better." He paused as if for a moment in deep thought, "'sides - they've got more money than sense over Chase Moors so serves 'em right..."

In preparation for the new job, they spent the rest of the evening planning who would do what, with whom, and where. Little Sam did some rough calculations on the back of a beer mat. The job at Fossey Woods had about two weeks left to finish, there was more clearing to do over the far side but that could wait till Autumn. They had better leave someone there to keep that job going. The elm trees work on the big Estate would take at least five or six days, maybe longer, what with site clearing and so on, and would probably be a three-man job, so there was the rub. There wasn't enough of them to go around.

Moira brought another tray of drinks over, their fourth, "you still at it?" she said to the huddled mass.

"'Ass right my darlin'," replied a perplexed looking Little Sam. "See - Chase Moor" he began "is gonner take us a fair few days, which means sleepin' over, and Pete prob'ly won't want that, Mike here says 'ee don't mind, but I needs to leave two blokes at Fossey Woods, just to keep the Ranger happy, which leaves," and he took a swig of beer, " just me and young Jonas for Chase Moor. Which ain't enough." He took another swallow. "'Ee's a strong lad an' all but even so -"

She interrupted him “well strikes me you've got the answer sittin' right there in front of you, Big Sam. 'Ee's a great big lummox an' no mistake, an' 'ee's worth two of you put together.” She turned to look at Sam, “no offence…”

“None taken,” he said with a smile, “I was wondering how long it would take for someone to think of it, I mean, it's not like I've got anywhere special I should be going to, and a few days here or there don't make a lot of difference the way I tend to roam about.”

Little Sam went bright red again, that was twice in one night. He looked at Sam, grinned, and said “well that's settled that then,” screwed up the beer mat and tossed it into the fire grate,
“'course, I don't want to cast no aspersions, but I was just waiting to see 'ow long it would take for someone to think of Big Sam as well. I don't wants all the glory, so thank you Moira for your assistance and get us a small scotch will you darlin'” and with that he smacked her playfully across the backside.

“You cheeky -” she was about to chide him but was instantly interrupted with –

“An' bring us a packet of crisps will you, I'm feeling peckish after all that brain work,” so that put paid to that.

She had a real soft spot for him so smiled sweetly back at him and did what she was asked. Ever since his wife had died leaving him with Jonas at such a young age with only a dad to bring him up, she'd sort of taken them under her wing. It must have been quite hard for him, for any man come to that, to have to get over your own deep loss and sorrow and yet to still be strong enough to carry on and look after an eighteen-month-old baby and hold a job down. She became a stand-in Mother to Jonas while he was little and one day she hoped, maybe, to become a stand-in wife for Sam.

He was a bit of rogue sometimes, but he had a heart of gold and was generous to a fault. She felt sorry for him at times but in her way, she loved him just for being him. He wasn't handsome or suave or anything, but you couldn't have wished for a kinder soul to spend your days with. She never pushed it though, if Sam Morley ever felt that he wanted her, she'd be there for him. That was the best she could hope for. One day he might even marry her but for now she was content to look after him and love him in her own special way. " 'Ere's your crisps you old bugger" she said as she threw six packets across the table, "one for each of you an' two for you..." Little Sam blushed again and young Jonas laughed. As she turned to walk away she caught his eye, winked her secret little wink to him, stroked him gently atop his head and gave him a soft kiss on the cheek, "it's getting late now Jonas," she said quietly, "you've all got to be up early tomorrow so don't be much longer, leave these old wind-bags to their beer, alright, it's nearly time for bed." He put his arms around her waist and hugged her closely, "alright Aunty Moira" he replied, "I'll just eat my crisps and then I'll come through."

She stood there for a minute or so with him holding on to her. She loved him like her own son. Sam watched and softly smiled to himself, the others all too busy and deep in discussion to notice and yet right there beside them a little moment of tenderness. It gave him a glint of longing in his eyes. Throughout all his years as an orphan the one thing he always wanted was a hug from his own mum. Probably Jonas was the same. A hug from his 'Aunty Moira' was always something to cherish. He was so little when his mum had passed away that he'd only ever known her in his life, and he loved her completely. He never called her 'Mum' though, always 'Aunty', but that didn't matter, she loved him like her own and he loved her like a mum.

On Mother's Day his dad always made sure he got something for her. Some flowers from the woods, fresh picked and wrapped into a little posy with string or a six-penny bar of chocolate, which she would always claim was 'her favourite'. Considering everything, his dad hadn't done a bad job of bringing him up. He knew his manners, was polite and always remembered his p's and q's and like his dad, would do anything for anybody quite happily. The only difference was his dad got paid for doing his things and he often got paid quite well. Very well in fact.

Sam was beginning to understand where all the cash had come from in their railway carriage home, stuffed into all those bottles and jars. Sixty pounds for felling a few trees was a veritable fortune as far as he was concerned and seemed like money for nothing. He would soon find out how tough it could be though. In the morning a new adventure in his life would unfold. Little did he know just what it would entail.

Chapter 7

At Chase Moor

The 'Huntsman's Arms' had originally been a coaching-inn on the route from London to Cornwall and was well placed as a stopping point when the first rail link was put through a few hundred years later. The mainline actually went by the village some miles to the north, so Tanworth itself was served by a long, curved spur terminating at the station which was built right next door to the pub. It seemed as good a place as any. Travellers in long ago times could stop off for a respite on their long journey West and so now could the new steam rail passengers. Have a drink, eat a meal, stay over for the night if the last train had gone, do a bit of sight-seeing, and generally enjoy the experience.

Sometimes the stopping train would be stopped a bit longer than it was supposed to as everyone would be enjoying themselves just a wee bit more than they ought and were not in any hurry to resume their journeys. But nobody seemed to mind. No-one was in any particular rush to get anywhere. Of course, it wouldn't happen with today's high-speed trains hurtling through the countryside at breakneck speed, intent on only one thing, getting from 'A' to 'B' in the fastest possible time. Never mind the comfort or consideration of the passengers, a card-board encased sandwich, a plastic cup of brown liquid that was pretending to be either tea or coffee only its maker couldn't quite decide and wasn't bothered anyway, or a cheese roll that you could use as a door-stop would be the best that you could hope for, but back then it was a different story. Rail travel was seen as a wonderful experience and opened up the far away counties and towns to ordinary folk. The age of the holidaymaker was born, and people could go further and stay longer and be a part of something special. Goods were trundled up and down the rails with ease and this in turn lead the way for wider choice, fresher produce and cheaper prices. Everything was great when the trains came. The railway breathed new life into a region but now this was nearing the end of the1950's and things were beginning to change. Beeching was on the horizon.

When the lines were closed and whole areas were left without any rail links it was a tragedy for many small towns and villages, what were once seen as golden opportunities and chances for prosperity, those dreams were now shattered and simply cast asunder in the name of progress. And so it was for the village, when it lost its' station a few years before the main line closed.

Some of the buildings were still there but others had been pulled down as they'd quickly got into disrepair. Standing in the small road alongside the Huntsman's Arms you could still make out what it used to be like. The main building which originally would have been the ticket-hall and gateway to the platforms was now in the hands of a local coal merchants' and housed their offices and various staff rooms. The station-masters office, being the grandest, was now the Managers office, complete with brass nameplate *"Peabody Coal & Coke Head Office - Mr Peabody, Gen.Mngr"* although now it had lost some of its grandeur as the paintwork was chipped and peeling. Where the platforms and track used to be was now their coal-yard and the large empty frontage of the station was now their car park.

The signal box that was a few yards down the line past the end of the platform concourse had now gone, apparently someone had offered to dismantle and take it away when it was due for demolition and Peabody's didn't mind as they wanted shot of it anyway to make space for their lorries. It turned out the chap was a steam enthusiast, and he had this romantic notion to rebuild it in his back garden 'to preserve the heritage of a bygone age' he had told the local paper when they had covered the story. And then there were two first-class carriages that had been shunted onto the sidings, left stranded rather ignominiously on a short stretch of rail unable to go anywhere ever again, trapped for all time on their own little bit of track. They were bought by Sam Morley & Son, Woodcutters and Forestry Management Specialists.

He had a grand plan to live right next door to the coal-yard and offer logs and so on to any visiting customers who might venture past their entrance and at the last-minute change their minds and buy his logs instead of their coal, seeing as how he was much cheaper, but like all grand plans it never amounted to much. That was his excuse for buying them anyway but folk in the village knew otherwise.

They knew that since his wife had died leaving him with baby Jonas to look after the best thing for him was to be with Moira. She had always liked him, even at school they were seen as a pair, like childhood sweethearts but when the war came along, and he was posted overseas they just seemed to lose touch. Moira knew the story; he'd told her the whole thing one evening when Jonas was about four years old.

He had come back on sick leave one year, the summer of '43, he'd had a pretty bad time of it over there and was classified as shell-shocked. Anyway, he was in need of some rest and peace and quiet and within weeks of being hospitalised in the old school at Bexhill a young nurse had taken a shine to him. Like a lot of people in war time they never knew if they would ever see each other again and as he got better their fondness turned to passion and before he knew it, she was carrying their child. The trouble was she was a very frail young thing and what with rationing and the general deprivation of the era she didn't have a good pregnancy. His C.O. contrived to have him transferred permanently to Bexhill O.P. duties so that he could be nearby in case of any emergencies. They married before the baby was born and lived in a couple of rented rooms overlooking a churchyard.

The war ended and things got a little better for them, the baby was nearly two years old and doing fine, Little Sam had a job working in a local lumberyard and Rosemary seemed to be getting stronger with their improved diet, then tragedy struck. Just before the baby's third birthday she got TB and spent months in an isolation hospital on the outskirts of town. Like many others before her she never came out. He was saddened when she went but not uncontrollably. It had never been love at first sight. They were just two people drawn together by circumstances and when the baby had come along, he decided to do the decent thing by her and make a life for himself where they were. He hadn't really known anyone in Bexhill and after she had gone, he saw no reason to stay there any longer. He packed his meagre belongings into a hold-all, put baby Jonas into his pram and started out on the long journey back to Devon, back home. Back to Moira.

She was shocked to find him on her doorstep late one afternoon, especially with a baby in tow, and whilst wanting to know all the details, she held back and instead offered him the kind of support only a true friend could and welcomed him in with a heart-warming hug. He lived in one of the spare letting rooms above the pub for the first few years and when the carriages had come up for sale, he thought they would be perfect for him and Jonas to make a home in.

No one in the village thought ill of them living under the same roof during those two years, indeed most felt that it was what should have been, that they were meant for each other. They didn't sleep together at first, in fact not for quite a time after Little Sam had moved in, it somehow didn't seem right but slowly their mutual love and need for each other took a hold and they became a 'couple'. It wasn't as if they shared the same bed all the time. Sometimes, when he felt a bit low, when things were getting on top of him, lack of work, problems with baby Jonas, he was able to turn to Moira for comfort and she always found a way of pulling him through it. She didn't mind, she loved him, always had.

Not long after he'd first arrived back in Tanworth he'd seen a notice announcing a sale of ex-army vehicles over near to Bristol; trucks, lorries, half-tracks, bulldozers and so on and with all his savings went over there for a couple of days to 'see what it was all about'. A few days later he returned back at the pub in a three-ton camouflage-painted Bedford OYD truck. It had one of those canvas covers draped over a removable metal frame along the top and sides of the body, huge great big wheels and a steering-wheel the size of a dustbin lid, but best of all it had a steel hawser on a powered winch mounted on the front axle with a huge hook attached to it.

"You paid two hundred pounds for that!" exclaimed Moira as he honked the horn for her to come out and look at his prize purchase, "you must be mad" she said in complete disbelief, "they must have seen you coming."

"Jus' you wait an' see," he said with that silly grin of his spreading all over his face, "this'll be the makin' 'o me" and with that he promptly drove it around the back of the pub, through the goods yard and into one of the old sidings sheds.

He found some five-gallon tins of paint marked 'Property of GWR' but as nobody seemed to want them, he 'claimed' them as his own and set about painting the new truck a nice shade of 'railway station green'. The finishing touch was performed by the village sign-writer who wrote in beautiful gold scrolly letters '*Morley & Son - Woodsmen & Forestry Specialists Est. 1947*' on the side of each door panel and across the drop-down tailboard at the back. This was the start of his new life; his own business, a son to look forward to growing up with, and Moira, to look forward to sharing it all with.

Some years later when the railway link was cut-off, and the station was closed down, all the various buildings and general flotsam and jetsam were being sold off was when he took a hankering to the two Pullman carriages which had been shunted onto a length of unused track and left stranded in the field behind the pub. Once again Moira thought he was mad but, in his mind, it was the best thing he'd ever done. They would make a great place to live for him and Jonas, they were next door to Moira, and there was plenty of space in the old station yard for him to make further use of. They would be a good investment for the future he said, "best five hundred pounds worth of anyone's money" he said, "be worth a sight mor'n that one day - you see."

She wasn't convinced but it was nice to see him getting on, settling down and making a life for himself and Jonas. As long as she could be there to be a part of it, well, that was fine by her. He had more money than he knew what to do with anyway, so it probably didn't matter how he spent it. In his own small way, he brought quite a bit of prosperity to the village of Tanworth, one way and another.

"Come on you - 'alf past five, shake a leg."

"Oh dad, do we 'ave to? I'm still tired..."

"Yes, Jonas lad – wee'm gotta get up over to Chase Moor by eight an' that won't 'appen if'n you don't get up soon enough now, will it?" replied Little Sam to his sleepy-eyed son.

"And what about Big Sam - 'ave you waked 'im up yet?"

"No need Jonas lad - I'm up already" said Sam peering out round the corner of the door to the washroom, his mouth all frothy with toothpaste and a green plastic toothbrush in his hand. He swished his mouth out, combed his beard and brushed his hair, looked back at the boy still laying in his bed and said "there's tea on - hurry up now before it stews..." The poor lad. There was nothing for it but to get up. With both his dad and Sam on at him there was no point trying to put it off any longer.

By a quarter to seven they were all done and on their way. Little Sam had loaded up the truck with all their tools, Big Sam had filled it up with diesel from the hand-drawn pump tank and Jonas had packed some things in a box for himself and his dad for their overnight stay. With the two dogs hitched up in the back, and the canvas cover pulled over they were off. Moira had made them some bacon sandwiches the night before and left them in the larder wrapped in grease-proof paper. She knew that Little Sam wanted to make an early start and there wouldn't be much time for any breakfast so it was the best she could do even if they were going to be eaten cold. Sam himself had filled three thermos flasks with boiling hot tea, as hot as he could make it, so that it would at least take them through the first day until they could get their digs sorted out.

Chase Moor wasn't very far away, about twenty miles or so, but Little Sam was a stickler for punctuality and if he'd promised someone, they'd be there by a certain time then they would damn well be there by that certain time. Or earlier. On time, before time or on the dot, it didn't matter as long as they weren't late. He couldn't stand tardiness, even if that meant gunning the engine up and down every hill and valley between Tanworth and Chase Hinton without a thought for the suspension or the comfort of his passengers.

"Drives fast, your dad?" said Sam, his teeth rattling and chattering.

“Yeh, a reg'lar Speed Demon, 'cording to Aunty Moira,” replied Jonas with a big wide-eyed grin spreading across his face, obviously loving every minute of it.

Little Sam glanced at them both and laughed, “who me?” he said with his face a picture of childish innocence. Mind you, it was a good job he had put his foot down as they wouldn’t have made it in time. Although Little Sam knew the moors fairly well, he wasn’t that hot on the individual names of places, farms and the like, and despite being given directions to the job it wasn’t easy to find, but they managed it. Trouble was him and Big Sam were busy looking for a smallholding, a tenant farmer as they’d thought, and that’s what threw them off. The place turned out to be enormous; two thousand acres at least according to Sam giving it a quick reccé as they drove up the mile long drive to the main house, an original Jacobean Manor with at least a dozen or more other buildings surrounding the area.

“Hinton Manor Farm – someone prob’erly called it a Farm to avoid property taxes” ventured Little Sam as they pulled into the courtyard, through a double-fronted portal and into the carriagery and stable-yard. “Must be a blinkin’ Lord O’ the Manor to live ‘ere” he added. The stranger they’d met in the pub the night before appeared from the Keeper’s Cottage at the far end of the stable-block along with a tall, well-bred man in his thirties, obviously of military bearing from the way he held himself. Both of them walking briskly forwards. Little Sam held out his hand towards them, it wasn’t taken up.

“Ah yes, the woodsmen” he said dryly looking them up and down with an air of contempt.

"Morning guv'nor, Sam Morley & Son, as promised, at your service" started Little Sam in his best business voice.

He was blankly interrupted with "This is Hinton Manor Farm, I am the Estates Manager, Mr Cowdrham-Jones and this is our Game Keeper Mr Quigby, whilst you are on this land you will obey my every instruction and do precisely as you are told. Is that clear?" All the while this had been going on Big Sam had gone round to the back of the Bedford to check on the two dogs which meant that Mr Cowdrham-Jones hadn't noticed him yet, but Sam had heard the conversation clear enough. Before Little Sam could offer any riposte to the Manager's arrogance Sam appeared from behind the truck, his huge six-foot frame and fifty-six-inch chest creating just the right image as someone not to be messed with, or spoken to rudely.

"No need to worry yourself Sir" he boomed "Morley & Son, Tree-Surgeons to the Nobility offer an exclusive and confidential service tailored to your needs. While we're here you won't know we're here, and when we've finished you won't know we've gone. That'll be sixty pounds please, all jobs paid for in advance" he added with a complete air of intransigence about him. Little Sam was desperately trying not to laugh out loud, Jonas was pulling his balaclava down over his face to hide his own laughter and the veins on Mr Cowdrham-Jones temples looked fit to burst.

Given the size of his adversary though he knew the best tactic was to retreat. Not that Sam would have done anything to him, he was a pussycat really. He knew his size and appearance intimidated some people but really was just a gentle giant. It had the desired effect, Mr Cowdrham-Jones instantly became more sociable, promised them he would sort their money out by lunchtime and if they would like to follow him in their lorry he would show them where the job was, "I'll just go and get the Land Rover" he said "then you can follow me down to the bottom hollow."

As they drove along the tree-lined estate roads following the Land Rover Little Sam enquired as to where on earth Sam got all that malarkey about tree-surgeons and Nobility from... "sounded right nice to me, tree-surgeon, sort of posh, what's it mean though."

"I read it in a magazine once" answered Sam "in a big house up in Norfolk, 'Country Life' it was called, and in the back pages was this story about a specialist Forestry Commission inquiry into some kind of tree disease and a tree-surgeon was called in, some chap who worked on the Royal Estates, apparently they can operate on a sick tree, cut-out the infected branches" –

"What like a Doctor?" piped up Jonas who was by now fully recovered from his laughing fit –

"Yes, like a doctor, and that way they save the tree instead of always having to fell it. Which if you think how long it takes some of them to grow, must be a good thing." Little Sam agreed. He was so taken with the notion that he made a mental note to have his signwriting changed on the lorry as soon as they got back to Tanworth, "Morley & Son – Woodsmen & Forestry Specialists – Est 1947 Tree-Surgeons to the Nobility."

"'Ere Sam, do you think there's a Lord or some'at that lives here, what we're doin' the work for?"

"Wouldn't mind betting."

Little Sam's face beamed, that's all he wanted to hear

Twenty minutes later and they were at the elms site, the bottom hollow. It was described on the Estate map as a low-lying sunken area north of the hazel ridge and was natural rut for the deer herd. These days though there were precious few deer to look at as the heyday of the huntin' shootin' & fishing crowds back in the thirties meant they were long gone. A small herd of fallow deer roamed about in the far reaches of the Estate where much of the land was overgrown with heather and gorse but that was about all. Without any hunting parties to pay there was no need to support a growing herd and so at long last they were left in peace. Nowadays it was only the Game Keeper who went shooting and then only for humane reasons to cull the sick or the injured, or occasionally for the table. Probably the only sport-shooting left was for Pheasant or Grouse but that would have been done elsewhere on the Estate's acres across the more open spaces. Rich folk paid handsomely for their fun.

Mr Cowdrham-Jones parked his Land Rover and beckoned Little Sam and the others to follow him down into the wooded copse where he stopped by a particularly sad looking Elm and started to show them the problem.

"As you can see where we've cut a section out to have a look at, the trunk is virtually hollow. It's as if the insides of the tree, the actual timber itself has been eaten away."

"Are they all like it" asked Little Sam as he rubbed the rotted wood fibre in-between his hands turning it into sawdust.

"We're not sure, but these three are definitely affected, as you can see compared to the others over the other side" and he pointed to a ring of elms which were well in leaf and certainly seemed healthy enough. Little Sam said he would check them out before they left, bore a hole with a brace, take out a core sample, just in case. As for these three they were finished and the sooner they were felled the better, no telling how safe they were, especially in a storm, or even if they might infect the rest of the elm woods close by.

He wanted to get one down and have a proper look inside the trunk, split it down the middle, see if it was infected or maybe infested, "could be a bad case of termites" he quipped as they walked back to the truck.

"Well, yes, quite" answered Mr Cowdrham-Jones in a solemn voice.

"You leave it to us Sir" Little Sam continued "we'll 'ave that big'un down first an' see if we can't find out what's going on with'em."

"Splendid. Well, I must get off now – I've got things to do, and his Lordship will be expecting me with a report. I'll see you at midday as promised, with your money" he turned and sneaked a quick glance in Sam's direction just in time to see him unloading the tools, in particular a huge hickory-handled twelve-pound felling-axe. Sam caught sight of his gaze and smiled a generous smile back, all the while spinning the axe high in the air and then embedding it deep into a fallen tree-trunk as though it were a knife in butter. Mr Cowdrham-Jones gulped and swiftly made his way back up the rise and into his parked Land Rover.

“Thank gawd ‘ees gone” exclaimed Little Sam, “‘ere Jonas, shin up the back of the lorry and get them flasks out will you lad, I’m fair gasping for a cuppa.” Sam was as well but he hadn’t liked to mention it, better to wait for the boss to make the first move he thought. Jonas was pleased that his dad had asked him to jump up into the lorry because his two beloved pets were still tied up inside and he was aching to let them out. He hadn’t dared while Mr Cowdrham-Jones had been there, just in case they went for him and his dad got in trouble. As it happened the two dogs were quite happily just sitting there, half asleep, patiently waiting for someone to come and release them.

As Little Sam handed out the still piping hot tea the two lurchers were bounding about all over the place in the bottom of the hollow. Sniffing everything and cocking their legs everywhere they went. On the far bank a family of rabbits sat watching the daft pair chasing this way and that - up on their hind legs, their ears perked and their eyes bright with their little button noses twitching in the morning air trying to catch a scent of their new-found neighbours. Sam was savouring the delights of his steaming hot cup of tea watching all these goings-on and wondering just how stupid two dogs could be, what with their supposed hunting skills and their intended prey sitting not more than forty feet away, what a pair. Probably only go after humans he mumbled to himself.

“Hungry” called out Little Sam from the back of the lorry.

“Yes” they both called back to him in unison. “We’ll ‘ave these ‘ere sandwiches then, what Moira made for us – crispy bacon with tomato sauce – they're cold but it don't matter..."

It didn't either, Sam loved the way the butter had melted all over the hot bacon and then congealed again all over it when it had cooled down. It sort of added to the flavour, all the salty meaty greasy filling squashed between the two inch-thick slices of bread, especially with the tomato sauce squished in there as well; lovely.

Suitably fed and watered (even the dogs had been given a sandwich) Little Sam promised them a trip somewhere after work 'for a proper pub dinner' as soon as Mr Cowdrham-Jones had coughed-up the money and they'd made a start, getting that first tree down, so they set to work.

Back at Fossey Woods Pete and Mike had started their day as usual, strolling across the fallow field nearby where their houses came out at the end of the village and meeting up roughly in the middle of the woods in time to start work at six. Once again, the surrounding countryside was alive with the sound of birdsong. Blackbirds loudly proclaiming their territorial rights to any who strayed into their patch, rooks and crows loudly hacking and cawing at each other as if in anger and tiny swallows and swifts delightfully twittering high up in the air above the fields searching for insects on the wind, sounding like a bunch of wild budgerigars darting this way and that.

But with all that, something was different. Something wasn't quite right. Mike couldn't put his finger on it, but he knew something was up. Perhaps it was because Jonas and his two rowdy mascots weren't there. Or maybe it was something else, whatever it was, it didn't get any better as they worked and when Pete's wife Trisha arrived later with his lunch it didn't get any clearer. It was as if he had gotten out of the wrong side of the bed that morning as he'd hardly said two words to Mike the whole time since they'd started work. Maybe they'd had a row, Trisha's arrival was just as silent and moody. Mike found himself eating alone as the two of them wandered off deep into the woods.

He also found himself working alone for the rest of the day as Pete never returned. "P'raps they'm gone off somewhere's an' had a bit of hanky-panky" he thought to himself and smiled, "yep, that was it, with all them kids it must be hard to get any privacy together, just the two of them, and maybe something came over them" he chuckled. Perhaps they'd had a row and had gone off somewhere warm and quiet to make up. Oh well, who could blame them, must be awkward at times, what with all their young'uns wandering about the place.

Not thinking anymore about it he carried on till four and then decided to pack up early, no sense in flogging his'self. The boss wasn't there so nobody would know, 'sides he was lonely working there in the clearing all by himself and the thought of Pete and Trisha enjoying themselves somewhere under a beech tree fueled his own feelings and well, he fancied going home early and having a bit of a frolic with his own wife, now that he was all aroused and feeling frisky…

Chapter 8

Dutch Elm Disease

At Hinton Manor Farm they too were thinking of calling it a day, Little Sam had announced his need to sink a pint or two of cider before dinner and now that they had the money from Mr Cowdrham-Jones it would be his treat. Mind you, they hadn't found anywhere to stay yet so finishing early was a must. They might have to drive about the Moor looking for a suitable hostelry and that could take ages.

Driving back across the Estate and through into the stable courtyard Mr Cowdrham-Jones was waiting for them all smiles and gestured for them to stop. "I see you've had that first tree down already…" he called up to the three of them sitting in the cab "well-done, first-rate work."

"Thank you very much Sir, we does our best" replied Little Sam as he poked Jonas in the ribs for nearly laughing.

Big Sam leaned out of the other window to speak to Mr CJ, as he wanted to call him, "Excuse me Mr Cee' er – Mr Cowdrham-Jones", Jonas laughed again "do you know of a place where we might stay for the next few days? With a pub and what-have-you?"

Mr Cowdrham-Jones had visibly stepped back a pace at the sound of Sam's voice but on hearing his question, so pleasantly spoken, breathed a sigh of relief and then spoke, "why not stay here, on the

Estate. There's a farrower's cottage empty at the gable-end of the yard, you're welcome to make use of that." They were stunned. Even Jonas, who stopped laughing. "And if you're hungry The White Hart Inn down in the village do a fine spread, the landlord there is a tenant, tell him I sent you."

What could they say, it was a generous offer, free accommodation, and right there on the job and the money they would save on digs' would add a little bonus to their wages on Friday. "That's most kind of you Mr Cowdrham-Jones," called down Little Sam in his best voice and then slung the lorry into reverse and started to back-up across the yard to the cottage, "much appreciated".

The little cottage was one of a small, terraced row of sandstone houses with small doorways and windows, finished off with timber roofs clad in beige coloured sandstone tiles. Built as tied houses for the army of workers that would have been needed to run a House and Estate of this size a few hundred years ago. Nowadays most of those positions had gone, the First World War had all but finished off the notion of elegant country houses staffed by legions of subservient lackeys doing the bidding of their Masters. After the 2nd World War, the ordinary common man found a new order, a new way to live. Everyone wanted a bit more out of life and not just the leavings of a sometimes-ungrateful family of snobs. The old brigade of the upper classes suffered for their arrogance and domination; the working man deserved respect and an honest day's pay for an honest day's work, that was why Sam Morley had no qualms about charging the money he did for the job that he did.

It was highly skilled dangerous work at times and a hard day's graft into the bargain, "yep, this'll do nicely" he said as he led his motley band into the cottage which was gaily decorated with horseshoes and brasses of its former occupant's trade.

"Only two bedrooms dad," called out young Jonas who had already bounded up the stairs with the two dogs rushing up behind him, "nice big double-beds though, wooden ones."

"Right-ee-oh Jonas lad, fling our stuff in one and Sam's in the other – all right by you Sam?"

"Fine by me, as long as I can get my head down, I'll sleep anywhere" replied Sam.

"Right then, we'll have a quick wash and brush-up and see if we can't find this 'ere White Hart Inn what Mr Cowdra-what's-it said about." Jonas laughed.

Two miles down the single-track road which led across the top of the moor they found the pub and right enough the food was delicious. "Not as good as Moira's but not bad really, considering," whispered Little Sam as they finished eating and ordered another round. With two pints of cider in him and a belly-full of steak & kidney pudding with mash, peas, and carrots he was beginning to settle-in to the atmosphere of this cosy little inn high up on top of the Chase Moor valley.

In a lot of ways, he was just like Sam, friendly and affable, able to talk to strangers with ease as though he'd known them for years. When he said what it was they were doing over this way and where they were working, several of the gathered regulars voiced a few mumbles and grumbles about it. How the Manor would never be the same again and how it was a shame how the new Lord had started treating the place since his old Lordship had passed away leaving the place in disarray and needing lots of repairs and a fair whack of money being spent on it.

"Them death duties 'll do for you every time," said Little Sam remarking that it was sad how these lovely old stately homes often had to be sold off just to pay someone's taxes and wondered what the pub folk meant. Mr Cowdrham-Jones was alright, once you got past the ex-military manners of the man, he was a decent enough sort so hopefully the new Lord was as well, allowing them to stay on the Estate rent free.

Some of the locals, joyfully accepting another round of drinks paid for by Little Sam, pointed out that Captain Jones was only a hired-hand when all was said-and-done and that the real owners were the ones to watch. There was a mass of speculation amongst the throng as to what was actually going to become of the place; a shooting lodge again, or a hotel, or one of those new-fangled golf clubs, but nobody really knew for sure, they were just guessing. It didn't bother Little Sam, he didn't live there so why should it, and anyway, he was being paid good money for his services so wasn't going to join in the slanging match. For all anyone knew it was going to be a grand stately home again once it was all tidied-up.

They had another pint each after that and decided to call it a day, Jonas was yawning, and the dogs were beginning to slump their fat bodies across the bar-room floor getting in everyone's way. This wasn't Moira's place so better not take too much for granted thought Little Sam, didn't want to upset nobody, besides, they had another hard day ahead of them again in the morning so it wouldn't hurt to go to bed early, and anyway, probably wouldn't get a wink of sleep, sleeping in a strange bed 'an all.

The old Bedford thundered into life and dutifully transported the weary trio back through the darkness along the thin winding moor-top roads as if under supervision from an unseen hand, a guiding influence keeping a watchful eye on its occupants. Little Sam needn't have worried about fitful sleeping, they were all three of them snoozing away as soon as their heads touched the pillows. In the calm silence of the warm summer's evening an elephant trumpeted out soulfully and a lion roared; at least that's what it sounded like to Sam as he dozed off. Was he dreaming, or was it the after-effects of five pints of scrumpy-jack cider coming back to haunt him...

Half-past six the next morning Sam was up and about strolling across the courtyard looking for signs of life; truth be told, he was really looking for a cup of tea, or some means of procuring one when he happened across Mr Cowdrham-Jones going into one of the rear entrances to the Big House. Following along behind he found himself in the large Kitchen where a small retinue of Estate workers had gathered to one side in the Servants Hall and Mr Jones was giving them their orders and tasks for the day ahead. Various jobs about the House could be done by the inside Staff but the more specialised work like the tree-felling was best left to the professionals rather than the outdoor staff. He heard his own name mentioned and was pleased at the warm recognition afforded him and Little Sam for their fine speedy work yesterday to the effect that Morley & Son Woodcutters were staying in the

Farrower's Cottage and should be made welcome at the breakfast table if they should so choose. They were obviously hard working and could prove to be most useful in the months ahead.

This intrigued Sam and made him think that perhaps now wouldn't be a good time to walk in on them all, so silently swept away and back to the cottage for the others.

"Breakfast 'an all you say?" remarked Little Sam, "with Mr Cowdrham-Jones hi'self at the Head?"

"Yes – true as I'm standing here, it's at half past seven in the servants hall. We should go over there sharpish, don't you think..."

"I'm thinks you'm is starving again Sam old lad" he replied and laughed. Jonas laughed again as well.

"Why's you keep laughing Jonas?" asked Little Sam to his son.

"It's Mister thingy what's given us this job."

"An' what about 'im."

"His name makes me laugh, every time I 'ears it."

"What – Mr Cowdrham-Jones?" interrupted Sam.

"Ass' it -" he laughed out loud again like all fourteen-year-old boys are wont to, "it sounds like cow-dung don't it."

The two of them stood silently for a minute while it sank in then looked at each other and started to smile then gradually both broke into a full-blown belly-laugh at the thought of it.

"Well bugger me!" said Little Sam, "so it bloomin' well does... I'll never be able to look 'im in the eye again" he said with a grin, "you scallywag, thinking o' that an' laughing all this time."

Breakfast was quite nice. Not Sam's usual ten out of ten score perhaps, but pleasant enough. The cook, a local village widow-woman, a bit tubby but with a perky little smile, took a shine to Sam. They noticed that she gave him two fried eggs instead of one and an extra rasher of bacon. He didn't know what it was – either he looked all helpless with his straggly beard and curly head of hair that they wanted to Mother him – or his large chest and broad shoulders aroused some secret passions in them that they just wanted to fall into his arms all dreamily and be carried off to distant lands. Still, he wasn't complaining, after a night on the beer a good breakfast was a must.

When they went to leave, she'd made-up a flask of tea, "I'll send a boy out later with some cheese rolls an' such if you do like" she said as she handed Sam the Thermos, "just so's you don't go hungry."

"That's very kind of you my dear" he replied with a smile and turned to leave. As they passed through the kitchen door back into the courtyard she winked at him.

"You've cracked it there, Sam old lad" laughed Little Sam as they walked across to the lorry and made their way out into the stable yard and off to the Bottom Hollow.

The job at Fossey Woods had been going for a couple of hours already as it was by now getting on for quarter-past eight but in that time, Pete had hardly spoken two words to Mike. It wasn't anger or a sullen silence, it was just as if he was 'somewhere else'. It didn't bother Mike that much to start with – he'd been walking around all morning with that inane grin on his face which signals to all and sundry that he'd had a lovely night of passion with Doreen but by now it was beginning to wear a bit thin. He resolved himself to ignore it and just carried on cutting and clearing, having a fag now and then and planning to stop for a tea-break in an hour or so.

The coppicing that had been practised in the Fossey throughout the years had resulted in some fine tall hazel and birch poles growing; straight as an arrow and ideal for fence poles and withy's. That was the beauty about this kind of work; in the first instance someone, a land owner or some-such paid you to maintain his forest and woodlands, coppicing, planting, clearing, felling, that kind of thing, and then with the spoils were all the trades that relied on the prepared branches, poles, timbers, saw-dust and so on for their own use. Fence maker's, thatcher's, charcoal burner's, basket weaver's, house builder's – the list was endless and for Morley & Son quite a nice little earner, especially when the average wage was only about six or seven pounds a week. That's why Mike liked the work, on a good day they could make maybe two pounds ten shillings, sometimes even three pounds so his weekly pay packet on a Friday could easily be twelve to fifteen pounds, more than enough for anyone, although it never seemed enough for Pete…

He was always complaining about how much his kids cost him, "they'll eat me out of house and home" was his favourite saying when the subject came up, so he could never be satisfied no matter what Sam paid him. It wasn't that he didn't enjoy the work – far from it, he loved the freedom, working outdoors, the perks of working for a likable rogue like Sam Morley – free lunches and all the beer you could drink, but he just had this bug about things, a chip' on his shoulder. If it was 'Pete Williams & Sons' he would have been a lot happier, all the money would have been his and he'd be the rich 'millionaire'.

Like all the people who think like this they almost never get their dream; they never get off their backsides and do anything about it. They spend their whole lives grumbling about it and how nobody ever gives them a chance, how 'luck' never taps them on the shoulder. It was sad really because that kind of resentful bitterness eats away at you and then one day something snaps and you can't take it anymore, you wake up one morning and do something rash and probably regret it the rest of your life. So, it was with Pete.

About half-way through the morning, he suddenly stopped work, downed tools and said he was off. Mike asked where he was going and got the reply to 'mind his own business' and 'by the way, Trisha wouldn't be out today with any lunch, so you'll have to make do, she's got something on, an' I've got to meet her after', which put Mike in his place and that was that.

"Well, I'm stayin' 'ere" he mumbled to himself as Pete disappeared out through the clearing, "I needs the money even if you don't, grumpy sod."

Thankfully for Mike his wife had sent him off this morning with some cheese and pickle sandwiches "to keep you goin' my lover" so when it came to midday at least he wouldn't go hungry.

"Shame about Trish not coming" he thought to himself, still, with the way Pete had been acting these last two or three days perhaps something was up. Not one to ponder too much on life's vicissitudes he just carried on, did a decent day's work and promised himself a pint at the Huntsman' on the way home. With the chimes of evensong echoing across the meadows and the blackbirds saying goodnight to everyone in a final burst of song he decided to call it a day. He'd made a good pile of hazel poles, stripped some lovely silver-birch and logged-up a few baskets of old fallen oak, not bad for a day's work – so the sight of Moira pumping a fine dark ale into his favourite jug was most welcome.

"Has he phoned?" enquired Mike whilst pausing for a breath in-between gulps.

"Yes, about an hour ago. 'Ee said if you and Pete came in hungry or thirsty then the drinks were on 'im, so put your money away," she replied with a smile.

Another swallow and half a pint was gone already, "don't know about that, Pete buggered-off a'fore lunch time, don't know where 'ee went, mumbled sump'thin 'bout meeting Trisha and to mind me own business." Moira stood and listened. "So, I just did me work an' that were that; cep'tin I'm starving, only 'ad a cheese and pickle sandwich all day, don't spose you got any o' them pasties left? I'll eat one o' them a'fore me tea if'n you 'ave."

She always did. Moira was like that. Always had plenty of food ready, even during the war, she never went short. Everyone in the village used to bring their surplus food and what-have-you to the pub where it could be stored out of harm's way down in the cellar. They'd had a Parish Council meeting one particularly dark winter and decided that if the village were to get bombed or blown-up or attacked by Germans, then the safest place to store vital supplies would be Moira's cellar. If anything was going to happen in Tanworth then they'd be ready for it. "Be prepared" as the village postmaster had said, proudly putting two fingers to his forehead and making the boy scout salute of his youth. It also meant that if any family were having a hard time of it, they could go to the pub and have a share out from the store to keep them going, everyone chipped in and everyone benefited. Folk worked together in Tanworth during those dark despairing years and when Sam Morley – local lad and trained woodsman – came back the tradition sort of carried on.

He gave jobs to people who needed them most, helped to re-build the village hall where they could meet and hold dances, play bingo on a Friday, sorted some new huts for the school and generally spread his good fortune all around, and of course gave Moira anything she wanted. With his particular skills he was never short of work; so much re-building was needed after the war that the sawmills kept him quite busy for timber and the like and the money just piled up. People in the village knew this but no one had been resentful, they all knew that one way or another they had all benefited from his being amongst them and no one begrudged him his success. Until now…

That evening his railway carriage home was broken into. The next morning Constable Melcombe was called and said that he couldn't make out if anything was missing; the place was such a shambles anyway you'd never notice if something had been taken, but Moira knew. She knew there'd long been a particularly strange item of bric-a-brac sitting on top of the sideboard which was always stuffed with money and now wasn't there anymore.

"The gold-fish bowl's gone," she said, "just by there, you can see the ring of dust where it used to be…" and she pointed at the sideboard.

That was it then. A robbery. Someone had crept out here in the dead of night, probably put a sack against a window to muffle the sound and broken the glass with a brick or a hammer or something, then stolen the goldfish bowl full of pound notes and fivers, that was how the Constable saw it.

"I'll 'ave to drive over the moors later today and fetch young Samuel back, 'ee'll 'ave to go over the place – see if anything else is missing – make a statement," he continued, "so if you'll give me the address Mrs Thompson then I'll be off."

"Certainly Constable Melcombe," she said, being all official and correct, after all, this was the first robbery they'd had in the village for nigh on twenty years and the fact that it was her Little Sam who was robbed made it all the more serious. "Hinton Manor Farm, Lower Buckton, Chase Moors, Devon" she solemnly read out to the policeman; "telephone Buckton five, two, four."

"I'll not telephone, it's too important, I shall drive there myself, in person."

Moira agreed. With Sam's jolly nature it'd be the last thing he would be expecting, and anyway, for all they knew the job could be miles away from the Manor and someone would have to go and fetch him so it just wouldn't be right to break the news to him in that manner. Far better to go there everyone agreed.

It was a pity about the robbery though, as the three of them had had a good time on their second day at the Manor Farm and the fast-approaching news would put a dampener on things. The next elm was down and disappearing fast on the huge burning pyre at the edge of the Hollow and the happy trio were looking forward to another pleasant evening at the White Hart. Well, the two Sam's; both Big and Little; were looking forward to it, a pie and a pint or two, and young Jonas was looking forward to a bottle of fizzyade and some chips. Big Sam had promised to lead them all in a singsong of some of his less bawdy country-songs. All was well with the world and yet within the hour the ess-aitch-one-tee would hit the fan. If only folk could see into the future, then all these nasty shocks and problems could be avoided. If only…

Their day had started bright and early as usual, the two Sam's and the boy with his two dogs running and leaping about his ankles like a pair of daft puppies, rather than a couple of ten stone lumps of muscle and teeth; all wandering joyfully across the courtyard from their little farrowers cottage and into breakfast with the rest of the Estate staff.

Mr Cowdrham-Jones, now getting to know them a lot better and realising that Sam wasn't really the sort to rip his head off, walked over with his customary cup of tea, two slices of buttered toast and marmalade and sat down at their table.

"I noticed quite a plume of smoke rising from the Hollow yesterday…"

"'Ass right," replied Little Sam in between mouthfuls of scrambled-egg and bacon, "them elms' is diseased an' I don't want any o' the timber getting out across't the county, never know where it might spread."

"Oh, I see."

"Best not take any chances – safest to burn it all up till I knows what it is."

"Fine, I quite understand, we wouldn't want the rest of the Estate infected, particularly when the next shipment of animals arrives."

As the man drank his tea and spread his toast Little Sam looked up at him, "shame though – I usually makes a bob or two from the old timber lark," and burst out laughing. For a man who was paying £60.00 Mr Cowdrham-Jones smiled, nodded, and with a slight lift of his head in acknowledgement of Little Sam's jocularity carried on eating. After a while he left to address the Staff on their day's chores.

"Did he say animals?" piped up young Jonas as they finished up and began to make their way out into the early morning sunshine.

A couple of hours later Little Sam had topped off another elm and he and Sam were beginning to make ready for felling the main trunk. Although he was a big man and had done a fair bit of lumber-work in the past he was prepared to leave the big chainsaw work to his namesake. It was rather a mean looking monster of a chainsaw; a petrol driven ex-Army surplus job that Little Sam had picked up on his travels, from yet another auction over Bristol way probably, but in his expert hands could cut through a tree like a knife through butter. The two smaller chainsaws with their tiny two-stroke engines were much friendlier to use and both Big Sam and Jonas could happily use them to lop off side branches once the main trunk was down.

The preparations for felling a fully-grown tree were religiously followed; line of fall, safety of workers, possible damage to surrounding trees at the moment of falling, all these things had to be taken into account. You couldn't just slice through a trunk, shout 'timber' and hope for the best. Little Sam had his quirky little ways of doing things, his routines that he would avidly follow without fail and his superstitious little rituals.

First, he would get Jonas to lay out three sticks on the ground, like an arrow pointing the way that it would fall, and then to the delight of the boy he'd try his hardest to aim for it and land right on top of them. Next he would get him to send the dogs off, barking and growling and running about the place like demented Visigoths which would clear any animals or humans from the danger zone then he'd clack his football-fans slapper-stick for several minutes to frighten off any birds or squirrels that might be innocently perching in the tree he was about to topple, and then finally he'd spit into the wind to see which way it was blowing, blow a long ear-piercingly shrill whistle on his old school-masters pea-whistle and start up the motor. At that moment the noise would be so deafening that anything left in his line of sight still standing was either stupid or inanimate so the sawing could begin. A few minutes later the shout of 'timber' went up and the tree was falling.

It always seemed a shame to cut down these grand old trees, they'd probably taken a couple of hundred years or so to get this big but when they were diseased and dangerous like these elms there was nothing else for it. Little Sam had, as an afterthought, decided to keep a small cross-section from each trunk before they burnt it so that he could hand them over to the Man from The Ministry for investigation. The Forestry Commission would have to be told as well, just in case it was something to be worried about, rather than a simple local occurrence.

The two dogs were still doing their 'get out of the way' stuff all about the place while the three of them had a quick sup of tea from the cook's thermos flask.

It just about lasted till mid-afternoon without going too cold and was most welcome. Little Sam grinned each time it was opened; the thought of the dumpy little cook back at the Estate kitchen taking a shine to Big Sam made him laugh. They were just contemplating finishing off for the day when in the distance they could hear the sound of a motor-car engine approaching. Standing up in the back of the lorry to get a better look Jonas announced it was a police car, coming up the single-track road, with Mr Cowdrham-Jones leading the way in his Land Rover.

"Dad! dad – it looks like Constable Melcombe in his old Austin 16 police car – coming this way!"

"Cousin Donald," said Little Sam, "what's 'ee doin' 'ere?"

"You don't think there's anything wrong with Aunty Moira, do you Dad?" said a worried little boy as he clambered down the back of the lorry.

Sam moved to catch him as he jumped off the back-plate, "nothing like that young Jonas, you'll see, probably your dad's won the Pools or something," and laughed, trying to keep the boy's spirits up, "and anyway, he hasn't got his bell ringing so it can't be that much of a panic."

Within minutes the two vehicles pulled-up and the occupants alighted, Mr Cowdrham-Jones leading the policeman across the track towards the ridge of the Hollow where a worried looking trio were anxiously waiting.

"Morning Samuel," said Constable Melcombe, trying not to be all officious and melodramatic.

"Morning Cousin Donald, what brings you out here?"

"I'm afraid I 'ave to report that there's been a burglary. Your Pullman 'as been broken into..." A sigh of relief went up as if to say, 'is that all'.

Mr Cowdrham-Jones stepped forward and spoke, "Is there anything missing?"

"A goldfish-bowl Sir," replied Cousin Donald calmly, to which Mr Jones nearly laughed, coughed and spluttered and finally answered "and you've come all that way for that!" as if in complete disbelief at the Constable's idiocy.

"Well, it did happen to contain over two hundred pounds in fivers and pound notes your Lordship," replied the policeman all matter-of-factly.

He glanced over to Little Sam whose face by now had got back some of its colour. He too had worried for a split-second whether it was bad news about Moira and the relief written over his face that it was only a bit of money stolen didn't seem to sit well with the policeman.

"I thought you would 'ave been upset or somethin' Samuel, that's why I come over personally" he said quietly.

"It's only money Donald," replied Little Sam, thankful that it wasn't his beloved landlady.

Mr Jones couldn't believe the calmness of the man who was going up in his estimation daily, "if you want to take a few days off Mr Morley, I'll understand."

"'Ee 'll 'ave to your Lordship – I needs 'im to come back with me an' check if anything else is missing, make a Statement – that sort of thing."

"Well, that puts paid to today then you two," said Little Sam to Sam and Jonas "do you want to come wi' me, or does you want to stay 'ere an' ave' a day off as well?" he said to them both with a grin.

"I dunno Dad," replied the boy.

"I don't mind" said Sam, then Mr Cowdrham-Jones spoke, "why don't you both stay here for now, we've got some tigers arriving tomorrow and I'm sure you'll both be fascinated to watch."

A puzzled look fell across all the adults' faces, young Jonas however had a big wide-eyed grin across his face like to beat the Cheshire cat, "Oh yes please!" he said.

"Right then, that's settled – your father will go with the Constable here to sort out this dreadful robbery business – and you two can stay here and in the morning, we can watch the new animals being unloaded." And that was that.

As they all went their separate ways each pair had a different set of thoughts to mull over. Young Jonas that he'd never seen a tiger before in his life and the excitement of it was making him chatter incessantly. Sam that he now knew he hadn't been dreaming the night before when he thought he had been under the influence of too much cider. And Little Sam that he was thankful Moira was alright and because he couldn't think who'd want to break into his home and steal his money. Mr Cowdrham-Jones because he was beginning to see these country 'yokels' in a different light, they weren't all money-grabbing schemers out to make a quick buck, they were hard-working, hard-living, decent honest folk.

And finally, Constable Melcombe, who for the first time in his life had a real-live crime to investigate, right there on his own patch, "that Lordship feller is a nice sort, very well spoken," he mumbled as he and Little Sam loaded the two dogs into the Bedford and waved goodbye to Jonas.

"Yes," replied Little Sam, "you wouldn't think he works on the Estate just like the rest of us, would you" and grinned that twinkly little smile of his as if to say 'what a twit Donald' as the old black Austin drove slowly away.

Two days later Little Sam returned to Hinton Manor Farm. He brought a cherry-fruit cake with him, freshly baked by Moira. Jonas was pleased to see his dad, he'd been having fun watching the animals with Big Sam, but it wasn't the same. It turned out that parts of the Estate were being turned into something called a 'zoological park' with elephants, lions, monkeys and of course tigers which he was fascinated with, but he'd never been separated from his dad for any length of time before and was missing him. Big Sam was pleased to see him back, not having much money and no transport to speak of except the three-ton lorry meant that they'd spent their evenings in the Staff Hall playing billiards and ping-pong. The cook had been giving him the eye the whole time which made him quite nervous although he was grateful for the extra food she dished out to them both of an evening.

"Aye aye Jonas," said Little Sam as he gave his son a big hug, "did'ja miss me… - 'ow do Sam."

"We're fine Samuel – how about you – how is everything back at Tanworth?"

"Oh – it's all sorted. It were nothin' – all a mistake. Anyways, enough o' that. Look, I know it's Sunday an' all, but I'd like to get that last elm down. Get the job finished. What do you say?"

"Ready when you are, it doesn't bother me what day of the week it is. Besides, I'd never have known if you hadn't have told me," And he laughed.

"Apart from that, I got a Ministry chap coming out tomorrow to test them wood samples I cut; he reckons he knows what it is we got here and wants to confirm it, said it was good what we were doin', burning it all. Some kind of fungus that they'd discovered like what you'd read about in that magazine, shrivels all the tips up and then destroys the whole tree, a 'elm bark' beetle what does it, burrowin' into the tree to lay its eggs, says it could be quite dangerous if'n it spreads, Dutch elm disease they reckon. It's a good job I went back, gave me a chance to look it up in me forestry books as well so somethin' good came out of it" and he winked at Big Sam.

They all jumped up into the lorry and made their way out to the Bottom Hollow one more time. The last elm was down quite quickly and was disappearing fast on the bonfire, the disease had left it almost hollow, so it was going up easily. Next it was the stumps. Whilst he'd been away Jonas and Sam had made use of the powered winch on the front of the Bedford and had pretty much dragged out the last remaining roots and the stumps, so they were all ready for heaving onto the blaze.

"Should be all done in the morning," said Little Sam as they sat watching the flames and eating Moira's fruit cake, "get them stumps finished with and a bit of a tidy-up first thing, then I wants to drill a bore into them elms over the other side there, just to check they'm safe when the Ministry Man comes."

Big Sam had brought his billy-can out to the woods with him this time and was using a small scraping from the main fire to boil up his kettle, "thought we'd have real tea today – as it's Sunday, can't beat a fresh cuppa," he said as he dished out the milk and sugar that the little dumpy cook had given him, "got some corned beef sandwiches here as well, if you want one," he added, and gestured to the two of them.

Jonas grabbed a couple and immediately ran off to feed the dogs, "I'll give 'em some of Aunty Moira's fruit cake an' all," he said cheerily.

With the boy out of ear-shot Little Sam started to talk about the 'robbery'. When he got back to the Huntsman with Cousin Donald his 'house' had indeed been broken into. Moira was right, the only thing stolen was the goldfish bowl but sitting in the bar were Pete and Trish Williams and, on the bar, the 'missing' bowl – complete with contents. Donald was all for arresting them both, but Sam said no, he wanted a quiet chat alone with the two of them. Trisha was crying softly, leaning on Moira's shoulder. He asked everyone to leave, including Moira, so that they could talk more easily.

It seemed they were in arrears with their rent, and the council was threatening to send round the bailiffs. Pete said he didn't know what to do and Trisha said she would die of shame if anything like that ever happened then when the bloke came into the pub the other night and Little Sam had laughingly said he wanted sixty pounds just to cut a few trees down, well it finished Pete off. All that money sitting there in those pots and pans and Sam wanted more – as if he didn't have enough to start with! So, they hatched a plan to break in and steal some of it, they knew the door wouldn't be locked so reasoned that if they actually broke in then everyone would think it was a real burglar, an outsider. All they had to do was take one of the money pots and their worries would all be over. They could pay the rent man, and no one would be any the wiser. Trouble was, for all their problems they weren't really a pair of thieves and as soon as they'd taken the money, they felt awful about it and a couple of hours after Donald had gone off to bring Little Sam back, they walked into the pub and gave themselves up.

They had been sat there for several hours whilst Constable Melcombe went off, worried sick what folk might think of them, feeling sorry for themselves, worried what Sam would say when he got back. Everyone in the pub had spoken kindly to them, Moira had promised that Sam wouldn't be angry, but it didn't really help, Trisha was holding tightly to Moira and Pete was sitting in silence, staring blankly into the fire.

Throughout all this Little Sam had listened intently to the story then with a soft smile he gave Trish' a hug, kissed her on the cheek saying not to worry, no harm done, then he turned to Pete who was staring at the floor now, and shook him warmly by the hand.

"Now, first things first lass," he said, all fatherly like, "I want's you to stop that there crying – it don't do nobody any good." She smiled at him. "An' Pete. I wants you to tell me 'ow much you owes them council wallers –now be honest wi' me Pete – if'n there's any dark secrets a'tween us now, I'd like to be told, alright!"

Pete nodded and smiled back, "a hundred and sixty pounds all told, that includes twenty-four poun' to the Gas man and fourteen to the Tally Man – for kids shoes and the like."

It was quite a considerable sum, even by Sam's standards and with the wages he paid to both Pete and Mike, although generous in themselves, it would take them years to pay it off.

"Tell you what we'll do," he suddenly announced after a few minutes in silent thought, "we'll empty that there goldfish bowl out onto the table and count it all up – see how much there is – then we'll call Constable Melcombe and Moira back in." Five minutes later they had two hundred and twenty-seven pounds on the table and both Moira and Donald and the rest were called for.

Little Sam beckoned for them all to sit down and as he did so, he gave Moira a little wink. "Right then everyone," he started, "this 'ere money o' mine I'd given to young Pete here the day a'fore yesterday so's 'ee could go an get some new tools; axes an' saws an' things, so it weren't stolen. That smashed window in my Pullman were probably some local kids, just throwin' stones and playin' games. Pete and Trisha's got a lot on their minds at the moment what with the kids an' all and that diphtheria is back in the papers again, so she's been a bit frightened." He didn't know if it had, he just said for effect. "So, you've got all flustered for nuthin' Cousin Donald, there's me money there look on the table, all two hundred and twenty-seven pounds of it – exactly what I gived Pete. You can count it if'n you wants to..." He declined. "So, it were a wasted journey, rushing over to Chase Moor and fetching me back Cousin, still, I'm 'ere now so ow's about a pint o' mild my lovely and drinks for everyone," he added as he grinned at Moira, deftly changing the subject.

"Don't know about that Samuel," said Constable Melcombe, desperately trying to regain some authority out of the situation, "it's not opening time for another ten minutes yet."

"That don't matter none," laughed Little Sam, and whacked his cousin across the shoulder-blades in that friendly manner of his, "you'm worries too much my old sugar loaf, that's your trouble," and he promptly strolled behind the bar and started pouring drinks all round while giving Moira a big kiss.

The look of relief on Pete and Trisha's faces was a joy to behold. When they came to leave a little while later Sam had bundled up the money into a brown paper bag and he pushed into Pete's hand, well they were both nearly in tears.

"It's only money," he whispered as they stood up from the table. "Now you go out of 'ere an' 'old your heads up 'igh," he said, "you only did what you though best – an' if'n I were you I'd get down to that council office first thing, alright…" and he gave Trish another hug and Pete a strong manful handshake. "We'll 'ave a little chat in the morning lad, sort summat out to make things easier for you both" and that was that.

As the evening wore on other folk started to leave until only Cousin Donald was left in the bar with them, he said his 'goodbyes' smiled at Little Sam and Moira, "see you in the morning then" he said as they locked the door behind him.

One last drink and Moira switched off all the lights and they both went upstairs to bed, "'ow about a little cuddle my darlin', seein' as 'ow I've 'ad a bit of a fright," he grinned up at her, "an' as I've come all this way back, seems a shame to waste the rest o' the night."

"You crafty old so-and-so," she said, "what am I gonna do with you?"

"'oo me" he smiled back at her.

The next day he went with Pete to the Town Hall and the Gas Board office to pay off his debts. He told him to forget it ever happened and next time he should confide his troubles to someone. It was always better to talk. Trisha didn't know how she could ever thank him, and Pete said he didn't know how he would ever repay him. Little Sam told them not to worry, he'd think of something, and anyway, they were right; he did have more money than he knew what to do with and sometimes he forgot just how hard life could be for a little family like theirs.

Just then Jonas came bounding back and the story was finished.

"Let's load up then shall we, an' what say we 'as a slap-up meal over at that posh place down in Chase Hinton, 'The Follies Fransays' 'owever you says it. We could invite that Captain Cowdra-what's-is-face an' 'ee can tell us all about these 'ere lions an' things you've been looking at."

A big smile lit up the boy's face. A fatherly smile of pleasure lit up Little Sam's face and a smile of gentle acknowledgement for a deed well done lit up on Sam's face, "best bib and tucker tonight then," he said as he packed away his old billy-can and kettle.

It was a good thing they invited Mr Cowdrham-Jones, or as they now knew, Captain Cowdrham-Jones, because he was the only one who could understand French and read the Menu for them. With his educated voice and him calling from the Manor they didn't have to worry about not having booked a table either; they were whisked in, no trouble. Sam borrowed a suit from one of the animal trainers who were looking after the lions, a big chap from South Africa with a funny accent and luckily it fitted him quite well. Little Sam had brought a change of clothes back with him from Tanworth for him and Jonas and Captain Jones was done up in his best Evening suit, with black tie and everything.

"Might as well make a splash," he said grinning as they all piled into his Riley Grand Tourer six-cylinder saloon, "a present from his Lordship."

It was the first time they'd seen him relax and it made a nice change to discover his 'other side'. During the meal they chatted about this and that, Little Sam said they'd be finished in the morning and thanked him for the work. Big Sam said he'd probably stay on for another week or so, if the boss wouldn't mind as Mr Jones had asked him earlier.

"They need's a big lummox like me when the giraffe arrives!" he laughed.

After a while Mr Cowdrham-Jones then asked Little Sam to stay on longer as well, "there's plenty of forestry work to be done on the Estate – and we've miles of fencing to put up. At least a year's worth of work." But Little Sam declined. He wanted to be back with Moira and Jonas in Tanworth working on his little jobs. They made enough money to live on. More than enough. Then he had an idea.

He knew of a family-man who'd be ideal for the post, he had a wife, and four kids so would need one of the bigger Estate houses to live in, but if one were going free then he'd have a word with this feller and see what he thought. He was a good worker and was worth twenty pound a week of anyone's money. Mr Cowdrham-Jones agreed.

If the chap was to be in charge of the new Forestry Department and could help in the upkeep of the Estate then it would be worth it, and he could have one of the four-bedroomed houses that were sitting empty behind the stables. "I believe the Butler and the Higher Staff used to live in them," he added, and so it was settled.

Pete and Trisha Williams would have a nice new home to go to, free of debt and no rent to pay and Pete could finally be his own Boss; 'Pete Williams and Sons – Foresters', his dream could finally come true. That night as they drove back to the Manor Jonas looked out across the Moors, "look dad – *Red Sky at Night, Shepherd's Delight…*"

"'Ass right son, gonna be a lovely day tomorrow."

The next day when everything was done and all the tools cleared away for the last time Jonas gave Sam a big hug and said he'd never forget him.

Little Sam shook his hand and thanked him for the work he'd done, "I knows we've only met you for a short while my old bone-crusher," he said, "but it seems like we've known you for years. Where you off to next?"

"Nowhere in particular."

"Well, it's a long road to nowhere… Anyway, if'n you comes this way again don't hesitate to look us up will you," and with that he put twenty pounds into Sam's pocket, slapped him on the back and said goodbye, "them's your wages," he shouted as the Bedford chuntered into life and slowly moved forward and out through the courtyard. Jonas waved, the dogs barked, even they seemed to be saying goodbye…

Chapter 9

You're not wanted here

The problem with walking through Dorset and Devon to get to Cornwall was that you couldn't follow the coast the whole way. Somewhere along the route you had to go inland and that somewhere was Exeter. A quick glance at a map of the area revealed the problem. The river Exe. If you had've kept walking you would have come across Exmouth, a pleasant little seaside town on the eastern side of the estuary. Across the wide expanse of water that was the rushing currents of the Exe hitting the might of the sea beyond and causing all sorts of turbulence and turmoil for shipping was Dawlish Warren. Another pleasant seaside town with the beginnings of a caravan site and some holiday chalets all along the sandy spit that was the 'land' on the western side. This marked the beginning of the 'other' Devon; less Budleigh Salterton gentility, more Torquay and Paignton razzmatazz. Pasties and chips, clotted cream and scones, Neolithic caves and pixies. But until there was ferry across the mouth of the river, you'd miss it all because you'd have to walk inland like Sam.

Trouble was he'd already walked inland to avoid the Exe and then gone even further inland to work on the 'animals estate' as he called it and now that that work was finished, he found himself in a dilemma. Did he manfully make his way back down to the coast again in order to spend the last of the summer fishing with Wally in Marun St. Davids, or did he give up on that idea completely and head straight through the middle of the moors past Indian Queens then on to Newquay and call it evens, decisions, decisions.

Mind you, sitting on White Hill Tor high up on a windswept Dartmoor outcrop, for two pins he could have given up on both suggestions and headed straight for the North Devon coast instead: Epton, Dewcross and Felmore. All of them perfectly nice places to aim for and all of them appearing favourably in his journal. The choice was mind-numbing. Well, it was to Sam. As a man who hardly ever had to make great decisions of any importance the last few days had been quite telling. He'd traipsed on and on through the misty rain that was a seemingly permanent feature of the moors surrounding the River Dart. Side-stepped Princetown, with its dark foreboding prison looking as bleak and menacing as ever, tried to have a brew-up by a small meadow brook and got moved on by an irate Landowner (no trace of an accent so no chance of being the genuine article) and to cap it all he had run out of fuel to power his little stove so couldn't have a hot cup of tea even if he'd wanted one.

But today was the day. He'd have to choose which way to go today, or he'd be too far in either direction to do anything about it. This was his cross-roads. Or his tri-roads as he wrote in his journal, short for triangle, as in a three-way shaped thing; do you go this way, that way, or the other way. Well, it made sense to Sam. At least for the moment he was out of the wind, as he had managed to find one of the little stone shelters which were scattered all across the moors, put up by ancient tribes for the times when the weather would get bad. And it could get quite bad. If you didn't know they were there you could die of exposure out in the middle of nowhere and no one would even know you were gone. Luckily for Sam he'd worked with some of the moorland pony-men before who made use of the little bowers at times. Some of them were descendants of old gypsy families and knew the whereabouts of quite a few of these old crock huts which was quite handy.

With his maps and compass he could generally find something somewhere and up here you'd need it; the prison wasn't built here for the fun of it. Not many escaped and lived to tell the tale, what with bogs and marshes to contend with. And in the winter months with all the rain it wasn't a very nice place to be. Especially if you hadn't had a cup of tea for nearly two days and were getting cross with yourself for not being more decisive... The old Sherlock Holmes and Lorna Doones and Jamaica Inns stories were written in awe of the bleakness of the place.

As with a lot of things in life, the pleasant times always happened when you least expected it. He'd had such a run of things the last couple of months since leaving Barbara's. The thought of never seeing her again had sort of gelled his mind into the loneliness of his existence. The childhood without a mother and father. The strange years fighting in the

War without a family to write home to. And now the future to look forward to without seeing Mrs Henderson.

He coped with it the only way he knew how, by walking and working. Thing was, he'd really been walking in the wrong direction all these weeks. Mind you, if he hadn't then he'd never have met up with the lads at Tanworth, never gotten to feed a giraffe all by himself, and he never would have been sitting in a damp four-foot by four-foot grass-roofed hill shelter feeling miserable and all sorry for himself. But just then the Sun came out. Really amazingly, powerfully, all singing and dancing like 'hey world, it's good to be back' type of out.

In fact, it was so bright Sam was for a few minutes quite dazzled and in his frenzy to dig in one of the myriad of pockets in his rucksack and find a pair of his old plastic sunglasses he dropped his journal, and it fell open to a particularly poignant page. He didn't see it straightaway though, what with the sunglasses and the sunshine bursting out all over and his eyes all fuzzy with yellow spots everywhere he looked.

It was only when he crawled back in to gather his simple belongings that he noticed it. It was open on the page where he'd left Barbara's at one side of Devon; the day she'd come looking for him way across the other side of the county at his fishing friends place, half-way down into Cornwall because her husband Fred had died. That was the last time he'd seen Walter and even then, they never got to go fishing together all summer like they always had done in previous years.

"Well bugger me," he exclaimed, "if that don't beat all" and as he stood outside the little shelter with only the kestrels and hawks for company, he let out an ear-piercing yodelling rebel yell, 'yodel-oldel-oldel-ayayhee hee'.

"Well done, God!" he loudly pronounced, "just what I needed, a quick kick up the old backside – an' the Sun's lovely too..." That was it then. If the Big Boss Upstairs was giving him signals then the least he could do was follow them, Marun St. Davids it was. Yep, good decision. No use sitting here any longer getting all mopey for things that have passed, got to get on and look forward to things yet to come, no use wondering what lies around the corner, unless you're willing to turn it... That was one of his 'mottoes' and he scolded himself for not remembering it.

As he strode purposefully down the western side of the White Hill Tor, thirteen hundred and fifty-eight feet above sea-level, he started singing, much to the amusement of a small gathering of scruffy looking Dartmoor ponies; "he'll be coming down the mountain in the Sun, he'll be coming down the mountain in the Sun, he'll be ..." It was silly how a little thing like a spot of rain could make you so miserable and a miracle how a ray of sunshine could have completely the opposite effect. He'd even forgotten about not having a hot cup of tea since the day before yesterday.

Some hours later his buoyant mood had waned a little as he was really beginning to get parched. Now more than ever he wished he'd topped-up his meths-bottle when he had the chance, back at that last village, but, well, some people give you the funniest looks. Especially when you don't speak the same as 'them do'. Oh well, just have to drink cold water then. With the plethora of little streams rushing and tumbling all across the moors aiming for the Dart' fresh running water was something he'd never be short of. He could have lit a campfire but then everything was quite damp still from all the rain, even with the sunshine, so it wouldn't have been worth the effort. It wouldn't be too far to the next moor-land village, there were several of them dotted about although some not even marked on his maps, so hidden and difficult to find were they. He just knew from previous journeys that if he kept aiming sou'sou'west he'd eventually come across something, he could wait.

By late afternoon he was beginning to have his doubts of finding anywhere before nightfall and so to cheer himself up again and to make himself forget the fact that he hadn't eaten since breakfast he resurrected a song from his memory to sing. It was about himself. He'd been trying to make it up for years on and off but because he never thought to write it down it never really came to much. As usual he sang it to the tune of *Barbara Allen* which always lifted his spirits; "There was a Man who walked alone, along the country byways, he never knew which way they'd go, over fields and highways" – "he walked all day and slept all night, and never knew where he was aiming, he wasn't much of a pretty sight, and dum de dum and something," at which point he was rudely interrupted.

“Woss all that bluddy racket!” snapped an angry voice from behind a hedge.

Sam stopped in his tracks, “I beg your pardon?” he said, looking for the source of the outburst.

“You ‘eard – all that bluddy stoopid singing – it’ll put my geese of’n their layin’.” A scruffy, unkempt, smelly looking woman appeared through a gully. She’d forced herself through a gap in the hedge which wasn’t strictly speaking a gap at all, more a thin bit of growth in the hedgerow. He wondered if that’s where the phrase ‘dragged through a hedge backwards’ had got its name from, as she certainly looked like it.

He wanted to laugh but daren’t, she was obviously not in the mood for any of Sam Bishop’s usual joviality, “sorry about that my dear,” he said, and politely doffed his hat. Well, he thought it best to at least show her some manners, somewhere underneath all that dirt and muck was a woman after all, “just sing to myself on occasions – to keep my spirits up.”

“Well don’t keep ‘em up round ‘ere, bluddy row, now bugger off a’fore I calls me ‘usband.”

‘Dear Lord’ thought Sam to himself, the poor man, married to that…

“Well, there’s a chance for me yet” he mused to himself as he turned to walk away, “I always thought I wasn’t much of a catch in my jumble-sale clothes – but compared to her I’m a Prize Specimen and she’s the bait!” He apologised for upsetting her geese and asked if it was far to the nearest village.

“Couldn’t give a sod ‘ow far it is,” she replied, pushing her way back through the hedge.

Right. Okay then. Just keep on walking and pretend it never happened.

He'd been following an old farm trail for quite a few miles, reasoning that it should eventually lead to somewhere but if the woman was all it could produce then it would probably be a wasted exercise, still, undeterred he carried on. After about half a mile he came across a man walking a small herd of geese, about twenty birds or so. He was just as scruffy and smelly and unkempt as the woman. It had to be her husband. He was whistling a nonsense tune, completely off-key and no rhythm to it at all, and the holes in his mouth where his teeth were missing made for a strange blowy sort of sound to the song.

Sam smiled as they passed, tipped his hat and spoke, "nice evening."

"Piss off."

Oh well, they were made for each other. He waited a few minutes as the geese waddled by and then carried on his way as before, "this track better bloody well lead to somewhere," he mumbled to his three feet of space, "and soon!"

Although the evenings were long and warm with the sun hanging in the sky like a big orange fireball it didn't seem to be cheering the place up at all. The long shadows were catching everything at just the wrong angle; everywhere he looked seemed to be getting all dark and gloomy. "Another hour and I'm packing it in," he told himself.

Thankfully he rounded a small hillock a mile or so later and there was a small village stretched out in front of him, and because he'd strolled in off the moors as it were, with no road sign to see he had no idea what the place was called, how big it was or what facilities it had, but it would have to do.

As he walked down the main street, he noticed curtains were twitching, lights were either being clicked-on or clicked-off; it was as though they were either trying to get a better look at him, or hide themselves away from him seeing them, very strange. He went past a pub, but it was in complete darkness, it started to make him feel uneasy, I mean, it wasn't even properly nightfall. Whenever he came across somewhere he didn't know, or didn't 'click' in his sub-conscious he always did the same thing, head for the nearest Church. Alongside a church would be the vicarage and inside the vicarage would be a vicar, you could always rely on a Man of the Cloth. In the failing light as the sun finally dipped below the horizon he could just make-out the outline of the four-corner pinnacles atop the perpendicular tower of an early middle English church, part Norman part Saxon, so he aimed for that.

Five minutes later he was knocking softly on the vicarage door.

The porch light went on and an elderly man opened the solid-oak front door. "Yes?"

"Good evening to you Vicar, I was wondering if -"

"It's Father," the old man answered, "I'm a priest, not a vicar."

"Begging your pardon your worship." There was a few minutes silence.

"That's alright," he replied, and as the light caught his face Sam could see a smile beginning to appear on the old man, "happens all the time..."

Sam took his hat off and lowered his rucksack to the ground, all its pots and pans jingling and jangling as he did so, "I was wondering Father if maybe you had some food and a little drink for a weary traveller?" Sam softly asked, "I've been walking all day from the other side of White Hill Tor, and I ran out of fuel for my camping stove," he gestured toward the rucksack.

"Yes, of course – do come in young man – such a long time since we've had any visitors, my name's Father Howard" and with that he beckoned Sam into the house.

In the hallway stood a big old Grandfather clock with the time showing on it as a quarter to eight although with the fact that the pendulum wasn't swinging and there wasn't any tick-tocking sound coming from it the poor old thing obviously wasn't telling the truth. Sam often wished he still had a watch for moments like these. Despite the offer of food and being led toward the kitchen there was no immediate confirmation that anything was cooking; no dreamy smells wafting up the passageway, no steamy vapours to breathe in and make your mouth water, nothing. Just a long dark dingy hallway and moth-eaten carpet-rug to walk on with a half-hearted twenty-five-watt light bulb desperately trying its hardest to spread some light and cheer on the proceedings. It needn't have bothered.

The 'food' was that mornings bread, already going stale round the edges where it had been left out all day and the drink was plain water, straight from the tap.

"I have a small block of cheese on the stone shelf in the larder," he proffered, "it will go with the bread if you'd like some."

Sam declined. He was many things, but he wasn't a scavenger, scouring the land for bits and scraps that people deemed fit to throw him. He had money in his pocket and could afford a pie or some-such in a local shop, if one was open. If he knew where one was. If he even knew where this village was. If he even knew who this priest was. "The bread on its own is just fine Father, and if you've a mind to pop the kettle on maybe we could have cup of tea together," Sam smiled in his most offertory voice.

"No chance of that I'm afraid, the stove is out till morning." Oh well.

Sam decided to wrap the two slices of bread into his knap-sack and make his farewells, not wishing to outstay his 'welcome', such that it was. "Is there any place here-abouts that a man might sleep for the night?" he enquired to his mousey benefactor, hoping that he wouldn't be invited to stay there with the priest. As an outdoor man the occasional night in a proper bed was an unexpected luxury but somehow the thought of what he might encounter in this dimly lit run-down little outpost of Christianity rather put him off. A nice warm bed of straw in a barn somewhere seemed right now to be quite inviting.

The priest replied "if you walk westwards out of the village about half a mile, you'll come to the gibbet cross-roads at the foot of Culhampton Tor; it's a bit steep but near the top you should see the remains of an old post-mill. You can sleep in there quite happily, I'm sure. No one will bother you up there..." His voice had a slightly eerie sound about it as it trailed off into silence but Sam being Sam took no notice. Things that go bump in the night were for city folk and townies' to worry about; he doffed his hat, gathered up his jangly rucksack and headed off into the darkness. Even the villages' streets seemed dim and dingy as he foot-padded his way westward.

The 'tor' turned out to be not much more than a sort of lumpy bit of a hill, undulating across the horizon in a vain attempt at imitating those of the South Downs' of Sussex fame, although it was obviously a good spot to place a windmill on top of. And being able to revolve the vanes into the direction of the wind on all four corners of the compass was a masterstroke. A pity it had been left to rack and ruin by its modern-day contemporaries, still, it would make a suitable abode for any a weary traveller.

Parched as he was through spending fourteen hours without a single cup of tea to quench him the fresh milk and water from the vicarage was welcome.

"Samuel," he said to himself as he carefully opened the creaking door, its rusting hinges groaning and squeaking through years of neglect and under-use, "this is a first for you and no mistake – sleeping in a windmill," as he stepped into the moon lit interior of the building.

It was too; in his time, he'd probably slept just about everywhere that a person could think of – and a few that they couldn't – but this was definitely a first. A shame it didn't have a roof... Mind you, the light from the new moon streamed in quite brightly with a lovely luminescent glow which made it feel quite homely, more than Father Howard's little twenty-five-watt sparkler could do to avert attack against the power of the night, and it was free to boot!

An old table and some wooden chairs were haphazardly strewn about the main living area which was at ground level to the door-way entrance. The actual gubbins of the working mill being built in-the-round to one side so that the resident Miller could be on-hand at a moment's notice to hitch the pulling-horse up to the centre-post and revolve the thing around as necessary. An old bed frame of oak sides and cross-slats was pushed up against a wall, probably kids using it as a ladder to get up into the roof some long-distant time past. In the middle of the floor Sam spotted a familiar sight, the remains of a campfire.

"Well, that's just where I'd have put it," he smiled to himself and ten minutes later was gleefully toasting two slices of slightly hard bread with a glowing dancing camp-fire flickering nymphs and fireflies out into the dark night air through all the little nooks and crannies of the windows and doors and walls. From a distance it must have looked quite spooky.

"Aahhh," he sighed as he savoured the first swallow of the freshly brewed hot sweet tea that he'd boiled-up for himself in the small billy-can, "like honey on the tongue," he mumbled to his three feet of space, "this is the life – and I'll soon have that bed ship-shape."

Like every man who had been through the war you could make a palace out of a cowshed if you'd a mind to it, never mind dodging bullets or jerry snipers; a good kip and a cup of tea could work wonders for your morale.

The day hadn't exactly been that great; it had started out alright, petered out a bit in the middle, faded away completely even after the sun came out for those few short hours and ended up dying a death in the village of doom, but now none of it mattered. He had a little bit of marmalade left which the lovelorn cook had given him as a leaving present from Hinton Manor and it was going a treat with his hot sooty slices of fresh toasted bread. As he wrote it all down in his journal before retiring to sleep, he made a mental note to buy some more fresh milk and butter and stuff as soon as he could. Oh, and some meths of course, mustn't forget the methylated spirits for his little stove. A shame that some folk drank it, poor things, it made him feel guilty every time he went into a hardware store or garage to buy it. Always did.

"Perhaps I should get one of them new-fangled gas cylinder cookers," he wrote to himself on the last line of his travelling journal about the place with no name...

An owl swooped in through the hole in the roof and sat high up on one of the rafters mournfully watching as both the fire and the new occupant slowly dozed off into the land of Nod.

When he awoke the next morning, the birds were singing and the sun was shining in, all bright and cheerful making the outhouse really come to life. It was probably quite early, about three or four in the morning maybe but once Sam was awake, he was wide-awake so there was no lying about the place, breakfast was a-calling. Being up so early meant that you could quite easily find lots of things to eat out and about in the fields and hedges. Mushrooms were a particular favourite and where-ever you had horses roaming – or in this case ponies - then you were sure to find some after a good drop of rain helping to make the grass all damp and fertile. Fresh laid eggs were an added treat, wood pigeon or partridge. Duck eggs were quite tasty and made a sizeable meal if you happened to be near some fresh water or marshlands. You had to check them all for freshness before you could eat them though, find out if they were addled, but that was easy. A bucket of cold water or some-such, drop the eggs in.

If they floated, they were bad, best to put them back where you found them, if they sank then that was fine, you could eat them. Considering the large broods laid by some wild birds, ducks can easily lay fourteen or so in one nest, then a couple taken here or there wouldn't be missed in the great scheme of things.

The campfire was soon alight and a sizzling frying-pan full of field mushrooms and wild chives was under way. A couple of stones to rest the pan on and away you go, breakfast fit for a King. A pot of tea coming to the boil by the side, what more could you ask. Well, in Sam's case some sausages and bacon would have been nice, a bit of fried bread or some more toast, just a few little extras, but hopefully he could get those in the Shop down in the village.

"In London Town..." he began singing to himself as he tended to the cooking, "... there was a girl – who never saw her loved one, and she would be, all alone at times, until he came a-calling..." It wasn't really *Barbara Allen,* he didn't want to get all maudlin for things past, it was just a jumble of words that popped into his head while he was working, "de dum de dum," he continued humming.

Sub-consciously it probably was about him and Mrs Henderson; the memory of her cooking breakfast for the both of them dressed in only that frilly see-through negligee was an image that often came into his mind. Her completely naked body shimmering like a mirage under the fabric giving the occasional glimpse across the smooth soft contours of her breasts as they brushed from side to side.

A magpie silently landed on one of the open roof beams and stared straight at him, "one for sorrow" he involuntarily said to himself while touching his shirt-collar, "that'll be a bad omen if I don't see another," he mumbled.

An hour or so later, or what seemed like an hour to someone who told the time by the movement of the shadows as the Sun arced across the sky, he was all done. The fire was out, his pots and pans wiped out with a clump of dry grass and a clean kerchief from his rucksack and himself washed and brushed up as much as he could muster from his diminishing water supply, and it was time to stroll back down

Culhampton Tor hill and into the 'unknown village'. As he entered the outskirts, he began to notice small signs of life appearing, movement here and there, folk coming out of their front-doors and down their garden paths, making their way to work.

A couple of young men on bicycles rode slowly past him on their way somewhere; to a coal-yard by the looks of their thick black donkey jackets and flat caps on their heads. Some children were quietly walking about the place in abject silence even though it was the school summer holidays. Other folk beginning to go about their own business.

He doffed his hat and nodded a pleasant 'morning' to a few who caught his eye as he made his way back to the vicarage, but it didn't seem to garner any response, "got out of bed the wrong side," he mumbled under his breath. Never mind, Father Howard was pleased to see him.

"Good morning to you young man," he proclaimed, although in all honesty he was only about ten years older than Sam, "it's going to be a lovely day today." Considering it had turned a bit grey and overcast like yesterday that must have been an optimists view of the weather, still he seemed jolly enough about it.

"And good morning to you Father," Sam replied, equally as jovial, as was his wont.

"How was the old mill house?" the priest enquired as he stood in his porch-way eyeing-up a small climbing rose that ran up one side and up and over the trellis work surrounding the door.

"Not bad Father, a bit draughty what with half the roof slates missing, but otherwise quite pleasant," replied Sam as he watched Father Howard intently choosing a suitable bloom to snip.

Realising he was being studied so closely the priest self-consciously smiled, snipped a single flower just under the bud and popped it into his jacket buttonhole, "always like to have one of God's little miracles close to my heart," he said softly, "to help lift my spirits when all around is doom and gloom…" He led Sam into the house and along the dingy hallway towards the kitchen, "roof slates missing did you say."

The clock still said a quarter to eight.

"Yes, been gone a while I should say, someone probably had them away years ago," added Sam, "still in all I managed to rustle up a fire and a bed to sleep in, so it wasn't too bad."

"Good – good. Well, I was just about to put some breakfast on, poached eggs, if you'd like to join me and then afterwards, we can go across to the Service together." Having walked down the main street Sam knew the village wasn't very big but the turnout for the priest's little church was quite sad. A few old men, a couple of mum's with children too young to be left at home and a handful of elderly ladies from the W.I.

Sam sat at the back in quiet meditation.

He wasn't a practising Christian in the 'must spend every day in church' frame of mind but he was a deeply religious person none-the-less in his own special way. He lived his life in the belief that, whatever came his way, whatever trials and tribulations he had to bear because of the way he was, God was always there somewhere. By his side, walking in his footsteps, or just keeping a watchful eye open, it didn't matter to Sam, he just knew that He was always there if he needed Him. Little was he to know how much that would be in the days ahead.

As the service came to an end and the pitiful congregation shuffled past him and out into the daylight, not a one spoke to him. Not a single person. It was as if he wasn't there. It was pretty obvious that they could see him as at one point when two of the women with children passed by they seemed to be averting their eyes in a particularly strange manner. One little toddler, oblivious to her mum's oddness smiled up at Sam as she walked by. Sam of course smiled back and gave her a wink and a nod. The mother saw this and snatched at her child's arm as if to drag her away from a wild animal, scolded the little girl with a loud "come here!" and glared daggers at Sam. He supposed it was his appearance which did it.

He'd seen it all before though. The sly looks, the whispering going on behind his back, the twitching of curtains, in shops trying to buy supplies. You could hear people in the queue behind him saying things, "where'd he get the money from, the likes of him," "watch your purse Elsie," and it wasn't only the women.

Some menfolk could be just as callous. In a pub ordering food and drink you could hear them whispering "lock up your sheds tonight lads; there's a tealeaf in town." Not everywhere he went on his travels did people welcome him in. To some folk he was just a filthy old tramp – a dosser, even a wino'.

You couldn't change them so he never used to try, it was easier just to move on as soon as you could, put it down to experience and let it go but it was sometimes a bitter pill to swallow.

Father Howard followed the last member of the congregation out and then turned to Sam, "sorry about that – they don't take very well to strangers around here. I should know, I've been here fourteen years, and these few souls are all I've managed to gather for my flock."

Sam sighed, raised his eyebrows, shrugged his shoulders, stood up, patted Father Howard on the arm and said "don't worry yourself about it Father, I've had worse. As soon as I've got the things I need from the local store I'll be off, and they'll never have to see me again." The priest frowned, he did indeed know what it was like for in that instant he recalled his first year in this tiny moor-land village with its close-knit community and interwoven families when he used to offer his sermons to empty pews.

There was no organist, no choir, not even a verger to pass the time with. He used to light his own candles and then put them out again when he'd finished. Sometimes he often wished he could just move on, but it wasn't to be. He envied Sam in one sense and pitied him in another, "let's go for a walk," he said, "and I'll show you around the village."

There wasn't much to see. A pub which looked like it hadn't been open for years, a village shop cum-post office, a ladies haberdashery with a decidedly old window display faded by years of sunlight and a hardware store in what used to be the old blacksmiths. Sam stood outside as Father Howard went in to enquire about 'methylated spirits'.

"They don't have any but can get some sent over, it will take a couple of days."

Sam frowned – the less time he spent in this place the better as far as he was concerned but the priest was smiling pleasantly and trying hard to offer consolation.

"You could always spend some time with me – there's plenty to do around the Church. Tend the graves, tidy the grounds, that sort of thing. Our portico entrance needs a good coat of tar-black – if you're interested." Well at least it would keep him occupied, and anyway, what could it hurt?

A few days extra on his journey wouldn't matter one way or another, "fine by me Father, I like to keep myself busy" he responded as jovially as he could manage, given his feelings about the place.

By the time the little church clock had struck-out midday he was well into tidying the graves in the tiny churchyard, clipping around each one carefully with an old pair of hand-shears. There was a petrol lawnmower in a shed at the back of the vicarage which would do for the larger expanse of grass within the cemetery, but it was desperately in need of a good oiling and a sharpen having been left unused and neglected since last summer. Someone had obviously tried to use it since but with not much success, the dry clippings sticking to its blades and clogging the wheels gave evidence to that, still, no mind, a couple of hours spent stripping it down and cleaning would soon put it to rights.

Father Howard brought out a tray with some lunch on it for them both, "cold ham, bread, and cheese with some home-made green tomato chutney – one of the ladies in the WI makes it every summer," he said as he called out the contents of the small lunch which his house-keeper had prepared, "and there's a cup of tea on its way as soon as the kettle is boiled" he added.

"Very kind Father, I was just about ready for stopping so it's perfect timing," Sam replied as he took the tray from the priest's hands and sat himself down on a nearby bench.

"My but you're a quick worker Samuel," said Father Howard as he sat beside Sam and looked across the churchyard at all the neatly trimmed graves, now clear of weeds and overgrown grass for the first time in ages.

"I likes to keep busy" Sam mumbled in-between mouthfuls.

In the distance the kettle started whistling its head off, "ah – there she blows," quipped Sam as the priest stood up and briskly started running off towards the vicarage kitchen.

"One lump or two?" he called out as he disappeared into the house.

"Two!" called out Sam to himself.

Minutes later the little man reappeared across the lawns with two steaming mugs of freshly brewed tea, "I didn't catch what you said so I've put two in – hope that's okay," he smiled as he handed Sam the drink.

"Perfect Father, perfect."

They sat in silence for a while just taking in the moment.

"Saturday tomorrow," said Father Howard.

Sam nodded in acknowledgement, ah well, at least he now knew what day it was. The clock struck the half-hour with a soulful clang-clang, "that's me done," said Sam, quickly finishing off his tea, "time for work."

"No peace for the wicked," called out the priest as Sam walked off to the potting shed to have a look at the mower, "oh, no offence..." he quickly added, realising how insensitive that silly remark could be at times.

Sam smiled. Later that afternoon the grass-cutting was going well with the newly oiled lawnmower and a happy, smiling faced priest was prancing around with a joyous spring in his step at the wondrous transformation taking place before his very eyes, humming a little tune as he walked.

The housekeeper had called back to prepare an evening meal for the priest but was adamant that there wasn't enough food for two, "that no good wastrel 'll eat you out of 'ouse an' 'ome if'n 'ee 'as 'arf the chance. I doesn't like 'im round the place, you mark my words - no good 'll come of it..." she mumbled as she took her pinny off completely refusing to do any food for Sam what-so-ever. Poor Father Howard, what would he say to Sam.

In the event he didn't have to say anything, there was plenty of food to go round, it was just that Mrs Oakley didn't want to be seen as helping the tramp out by feeding him anything. If Father Howard wanted to share his food with a wastrel, then so be it, but she wasn't going to assist him in the task.

Who did this tramp think he was, coming here all uninvited like and making himself at home, "we don't want folk like him in our village," she mumbled to herself as she wrapped herself up and walked off into the night.

A while after the food Sam bade the priest goodnight and made his way slowly back through the village again and away up to the mill. The pub seemed to be open, at least a light was showing through a crack in the curtains, so Sam decided to venture in, as he did so a sudden silence descended over the place, a couple of locals actually stopped drinking in mid-swallow, still with their glasses raised to their lips.

All eyes were on Sam. Not that there were many eyes. Half a dozen menfolk at most. No women. As he walked to the bar the landlord quite deliberately rang the bell and called 'time', saying a quick 'sorry' to Sam as he did so, but they were closing early tonight on account of the rain, and no, he couldn't serve Sam, so he'd have to leave.

"Fine, as you wish landlord," said Sam as he walked back out accompanied by complete silence.

That night it did indeed rain but that was the least of his worries. Someone had been up to the mill at some point during the day and had been through his stuff. Pots and pans were strewn about, his medals-tin was open, and the contents spilled, his journal was tossed into a dark corner and the little bit of money he had left in the old tobacco tin was gone.

Thankfully the pound-notes he still had left were safely tucked away inside one the myriad pockets of his great-coat, so they were safe. The bed was broken up in such a way that it couldn't be put back together again and someone had tried to start a fire out of the busted slats. In the gloom of the night, he did his best to concoct a make-shift bed and used his coat as a cover against the incoming rain. 'Just another bad day' he felt like writing in his journal but couldn't be bothered, the less said about this place in his memoirs the better.

The next morning, he gathered up all his belongings and with a lasting glance around the place to make sure nothing was left behind he made his way out of the mill house one more time and back down the hill into the village.

Being a Saturday, he noticed there were more kids about when he walked through the main street. He looked in at the hard-ware store; no, his meths wasn't in, and by the sound of it, it probably wasn't ever going to be 'in'. Father Howard tried his best to put on a welcoming face, but he knew already that something was up.

Some of the menfolk had warned him off – get rid of the old Gregory or else – we don't want tramps and his sort around here. It wasn't so much a threat as a sort of forceful request, but the priest tried to ignore it and beckoned Sam in for a bite of breakfast. For his part Sam never mentioned a word of what had gone on with his stuff. "Must try and get finished up this morning Father, I've a long way to go and don't want to delay things any more than I have to."

The priest breathed a silent sigh of relief, "that's alright Samuel, I understand."

About an hour or so after midday Sam decided he'd done enough work in this place to repay the hospitality of Father Howard's meagre offerings and told the old man he was all done and would be off. A morning being watched and leered at by a crowd of local children over the churchyard wall was sad enough but when a rock was thrown at him, he felt it was time to give in. They didn't want him in the village and that was that. So off he went. He wished the priest well and thanked him for the food and said no, he probably wouldn't be back this way again, making some excuse about it not being on his usual summer-time route but that it was a pleasure to have met him.

That evening Sam sat dejectedly in a home-made bivvy high up on the moors miles from anywhere. His three feet of space came in handy at times like this.

"Well Sam old lad," he said out to thin air, "what now?"

He'd arrayed out his belongings; it was all there albeit a bit smoke charred, and his great coat was mucky but otherwise it was all fairly intact. Would it be south, down towards Fowey for the last of the summer, meet up with Walter at Marun for a bit of fishing or shall he give up on Cornwall all together this year and head north. Straight up and over Exmoor, catch a boat across to Wales. He could get across somewhere near Porlock and over to Llantwit for a couple of pounds hopefully and then make his way round to the Gower.

Wales – it held some good memories for him and right now he could do with some to take his mind off the recent events in the village of the damned. His three feet of space didn't reply, it never did of course, but it was useful to be able to talk things out loud sometimes, sort of made you feel like you were doing okay, not going mad, even if the world around you was…

An Interview with the Author

Where did the idea for this book come from?

Having written a lot of short stories on and off over the years for my own enjoyment I suddenly had an idea for a full-blown novel. It started many years ago back in mid-1998 when I bought an A4 writing pad and a box of ballpoint pens. I had the characters and most of the storylines in my head and it was all I could do to get it down, writing long-hand. I couldn't write fast enough – the words were just flowing out of me quicker than my hand could get the ink down. Before a few days I had filled the first pad, 75 pages, so had to buy another. Several pads later and I had over 65,000 words and hundreds of pages.

Was it all in long hand?

I'm afraid so but it really needed typing out properly; as it happened, I'd bought myself a shiny new Hewlett Packard PC and Printer which came with something called LotusWorks, an early word-processor, so I started hammering away at the keyboard.

When was it finished?

In reality it was pretty much finished within a few months although all of it still in ballpoint pen so the only delay was finding the time to sit and transcribe all of that into the computer. That took a fair while as I only came to it when I had the spare time but soon I had reached the last few pages of handwriting and realised that there was going to be a sequel (as the story was by no means complete) so bought another A4 pad and wrote a couple more Chapters. These were to round-off the first book (in readiness for the follow-on) and I didn't type these into yet another new PC until last year 2024 (life sometimes gets in the way!) so while it seems a long time, in reality it was only about half a year or so all told.

Where did the link to the folk song "Barbara Allen" come from?

In my senior school one of my teachers knew that my father came from Pontypool in Wales and was a good singer, so I was automatically press-ganged into the School Choir. We had quite a repertoire of old folk songs (Johnny Todd - Scarborough Fair - The Skye Boat Song and so on) and of course Barbara Allen, which was my favourite. Coming from Sussex we had our local version of the lyrics, but I think it was the haunting tune that enthralled me (and still does...)

What about the main character; Sam Bishop, the wanderer, where did he come from?

Where we lived there was a small Franciscan Convent and as a kid, we could always knock their door for a "drink" of water or squash if we were out all day and getting thirsty. Well on quite a few occasions there would also be the odd tramp knocking about as well; they'd be given some food, maybe some old hand-me-down clothes, a new pair of boots and sometimes even a bed for the night if it was cold. That kindness stuck with me. We called them all 'Old Gregory' as none of us knew their real names, but we were never rude or nasty as to me they looked like my old Grandad, just a bit rougher around the edges. I always wondered where they went to next…

Did you base Sam on anyone in particular?

Strangely enough it was while watching "Auf Wiedersehen Pet" back in the day on the tv and seeing a big actor by the name of Pat Roach who played "Bomber". With his soft West Country accent (in the show) and his huge frame (he started life as a wrestler before getting into acting) I knew that I had the blueprint for my Sam…

Is there a writer that has influenced you?

The H.E. Bates' stories. They were so lovely. Some years ago, I sent the first four Chapters to a friend to ask what he thought of my novel, he came back with "...very whimsical, made me think of Cider With Rosie, The Darling Buds of May, that nostalgia for times gone by..." which was nice.

Well, thanks for chatting to us, it's been good getting to know you and we look forward to the sequel.

You're welcome.